CHLOE *by* DESIGN

Making the Cut

BY MARGARET GUREVICH

ILLUSTRATIONS & PHOTOS BY BROOKE HAGEL

capstone
young readers

Chloe by Design is published by Capstone Young Readers
A Capstone Imprint
1710 Roe Crest Drive
North Mankato, Minnesota 56003
www.mycapstone.com

Library of Congress Cataloging-in-Publication Data
Gurevich, Margaret, author.
Chloe by design : making the cut / by Margaret Gurevich; illustrated by Brooke Hagel.
pages cm. -- (Chloe by design)
"This book is also available as four library-bound editions."

Summary: In this compilation of four separately published books, sixteen-year-old Chloe Montgomery gets a chance to travel from Santa Cruz to New York City to compete in Teen Design Diva, a competitive game show for aspiring teenage fashion designers.

ISBN 978-1-62370-112-3 (paper over board)
ISBN 978-1-62370-680-7 (paperback)
ISBN 978-1-62370-291-5 (ebook)

1. Fashion design--Juvenile fiction. 2. Television game shows--Juvenile fiction. 3. Reality television programs--Juvenile fiction. 4. Competition (Psychology)--Juvenile fiction. [1. Fashion design--Fiction. 2. Reality television programs--Fiction. 3. Competition (Psychology)--Fiction.] I. Hagel, Brooke, illustrator. II. Title. III. Title: Making the cut.
PZ7.G98146Ch 2014
813.6--dc23
                    2013050317

Designer: Alison Thiele
Editor: Alison Deering

Photo Credits: Brooke Hagel, 35, 102, 232; Kay Fraser, 19, 51, 357; Shutterstock/Andrekart Photography, 147 (top left), nito, 147 (bottom left), J.D.S, 147 (top right)
Artistic Elements: Shutterstock

Printed in China.
092015   009214S16

Measure twice, cut once
or you won't make the cut.

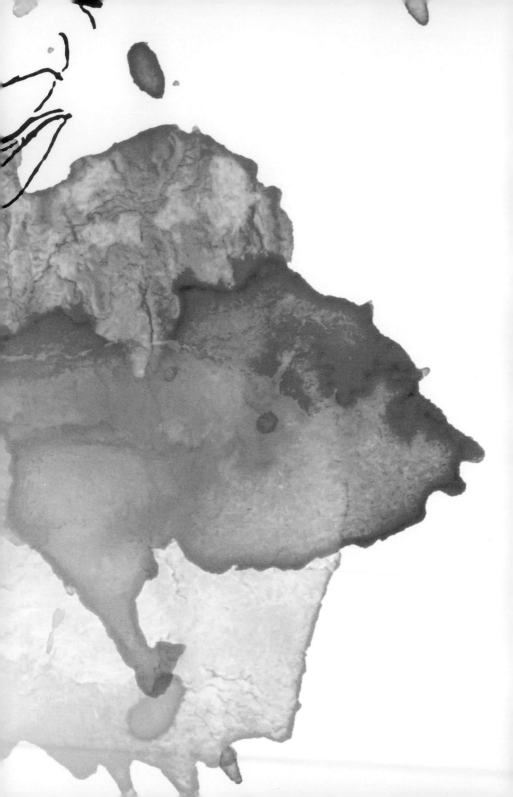

My name is Chloe Montgomery, and I am a fashion addict. There, I said it. I mean, I know everyone has hobbies, but mine goes past that — my interest in fashion and design is more like an obsession. Unfortunately, Santa Cruz, California, where I live, isn't exactly the fashion capital of the world. Don't get me wrong, it's a great place to live, but New York City it isn't.

Since there aren't many design opportunities for sixteen-year olds and I don't exactly get a chance to see runway-ready fashions on the street here in Santa Cruz, I take any chance I can get to soak up fashion. Enter *Design Diva*, the highlight of my week — at least as far as TV goes. If you ask me, there is nothing better than watching a group of designers battle it out for the ultimate prize: their own clothing line. Every week, the

Design Diva judges throw some new, crazy challenge at the contestants. Like having them design party clothing for dogs — excuse me, what? But I love it, and no matter how insane the challenge seems, I always have my sketchpad ready. I like to keep up with the competition by designing my own ideas for each challenge.

This week, the competition will be narrowed down to the final five designers, so the pressure is really on. Sometimes I don't know how the designers do it. I get stressed enough just watching from home!

Looking around my living room, I make sure I have all my supplies arranged for tonight's episode. Fabric swatches: check. Sketchpad: check. Colored pencils and felt-tip pens: check. Extra-cheesy pizza with crispy crust: check.

I catch sight of my outfit in the mirror above the fireplace. Tonight I've belted a flowing, black tunic over a geometric-print, black-and-white skirt and paired it with low black ankle boots to add some edge. I smile at my reflection, remembering a similar outfit the winner of last week's *Design Diva* challenge created. She described her style aesthetic as "simple chic" and the judges loved it.

I guess "simple chic" would describe my closet too. I'm all about clean, no-frills looks. I've never been one

for lots of loud colors and tons of bling. I'd rather use bright colors as an accent than a centerpiece. Give me navy, tans, blacks, and neutrals, and I can make them pop with a bright scarf, statement jewelry, or a stylish belt.

I glance up at the clock and realize the show will start in five minutes. Just then, as if on cue, the doorbell rings. I hurry to open the door, but before I can get there my best friend, Alexis (Alex for short), walks right in. Her hair is still wet like she just got out of the shower, and she's wearing an oversized gray hoodie and leggings. She kicks off her black high-tops — they're one of the only cool, retro things she owns, but I try not to make a big deal about it, because otherwise she'll probably throw them away.

Alex thrusts a bag of chips into my hands as she makes a beeline for the living room. "Let's do this," she says, heading straight for the couch in front of the TV. She plops down, makes herself comfortable, and picks up the remote.

I shake my head and smile. Alex loves *Design Diva* because of the snarky judges. As for fashion? She couldn't care less. If someone offered Alex a million dollars to tell them which shoes look best with which jeans, she'd probably just shrug and not even pretend to be sad about losing the money. I told her this one time, and she just told me, "I'll take the loss if it means I don't have to hurt my brain thinking about it. Besides, that's what I have you for."

Alex and I may be best friends, but we're total opposites when it comes to caring about clothes. I learned a long time ago not to push my fashion ideas onto her. But even though Alex may not care about which shirt or shoes go with what, her ability to think outside the box is mind-boggling. I can be stuck on a design idea for days, and all Alex has to do is look at my patterns and drawings for two seconds and boom! She comes up with some idea that works perfectly but is not *at all* what I would've come up with alone.

Here's a perfect example: Last week, I was trying to come up with an outfit for the school's carnival. I had my black jeans and a loose, sleeveless white blouse draped over my chair with a pair of flat black gladiator sandals on the floor. I liked the combo, but I wanted a little oomph. Alex opened my closet, stood there for about half a second, and pulled out my red-and-black paisley scarf. The same scarf I'd passed over for being too busy. "Done," she'd said. I had my doubts, but when I held the scarf up, of course, she was totally right. Poof! The outfit came together.

Alex was also the one who gave me the guts to start creating my own clothes. When I was growing up, my family didn't have a ton of money, and my mom used to take my clothes to Mrs. Murphy, this woman in our old apartment building, to make them last longer. She did an okay job letting out hems and waists to make my clothes last another year, sometimes two, but I loved the looks in magazines. I never said anything to my mom about it. I knew she felt bad making me wear the same stuff year after year. Instead, I watched Mrs. Murphy match colors, thread needles, take out one stitch, and put in another.

Eventually I started sketching and sewing on my own, but I was sure my designs weren't good enough, so I didn't tell anyone — except Alex. One day, when I was about twelve years old, Alex and I were at the drug store when I started flipping through a fashion magazine. Alex had leaned over my shoulder, set down the chips and soda she was holding, and picked up a copy of the magazine instead. Before I knew what was happening, she'd paid for it.

"Here," Alex had said, handing it to me. "Consider it an early birthday present."

"Thanks, but you didn't need to do that," I'd replied.

Alex had just shrugged. "Don't worry about it, Chloe. Besides, why should you be stuck wishing for these clothes? Your designs are good. You can make them."

I'd started to shake my head no, but Alex just put her arm around my shoulder. "Yes, you can, Chloe," she had said with a big smile.

Turned out she was right. And four years later, she still is.

"It's on!" Alex squeals as the *Design Diva* music starts.

I immediately focus on the screen. Barry Drayback, the host of the show, announces the judges as Alex digs into the pizza. First up is Jasmine DeFabio. Alex and I make faces as she struts to her spot at the judges' table. Jasmine is super hard to please, and even if she does like a design, her face still looks like she just smelled someone's dirty socks. You can tell all of the contestants dread her critiques — and I don't blame them.

Next up is Missy Saphire. Her judging style is basically the opposite of Jasmine's. Even if a design is ugly, Missy manages to find something nice to say. Everyone cheers for Missy because she's so sweet, but to be honest, as much as Jasmine annoys us, at least her critiques are spot on.

The last judge announced is Hunter Bancroft — he's the cutest one, hands down. He's also the perfect balance between Jasmine and Missy — nice, but honest. But if *I'm* going to be honest, Alex and I don't always hear everything Hunter has to say. Sometimes we're too busy staring at how gorgeous he is to focus on his critique.

"Tonight," Barry says, "we have a special announcement for our teen viewers, so make sure you have those pads and pens ready. I can't give away too much yet, but trust me when I say this is something you don't want to miss. This could be a life-changing announcement for some of our viewers. But before we get to that, let's focus on our latest challenge and our remaining five contestants."

"A life-changing announcement?" I say. *Design Diva* has never done anything like this before. "What do you think it's going to be?"

Alex shrugs. "Maybe it's a chance to have your clothes designed by one of the top three designers?" she suggests between bites of pizza.

"Oh, my gosh! That has to be it!" I exclaim. "You're such a genius. That's like the final challenge they had last season. Imagine if we get picked." I close my eyes and picture how amazing it would be to have one of *Design Diva*'s top designers create my clothes. Even if they were bad, it would still be fantastic.

Alex snorts. "If I win, you can have my prize. I'll stick with my comfy clothes. Besides, there's no need to jazz up the awesomeness of my ensemble." She sweeps her arms over her leggings and hoodie.

I laugh and grab a slice of pizza. All I can think about is what the announcement will be. On the screen, Hunter is talking about the fluorescent coat one of the designers made, but I can't focus on his words. What could Barry have been talking about?

I must have zoned out because Alex suddenly nudges me, then waves her hand in front of my face. "Hello? Earth to Chloe," she says, cupping her hands in front of her mouth like she's talking into a megaphone. "Come in, please."

"Sorry," I say. "I just keep wondering what the special announcement could be."

"I bet they won't tell us anything until the end of the show," Alex says. "They'll want to keep us sucked in for the whole hour. So try to focus. I can't make fun of the judges on my own." She grins and tosses me a napkin as a bit of pizza sauce drips off my chin.

"Gross. Jasmine would not approve of this look," I say, cleaning myself up.

"Speaking of Jasmine . . ." Alex nods to the screen.

On TV, one of the designers is holding up a blue tuxedo and looking ready to cry. That must be Jasmine's handiwork.

"It's not *that* bad," says Alex. "At least blue is original."

"What did she say to him?" I ask.

"She called his tux 'an homage to a bad eighties prom,'" Alex says, trying not to hold back her laughter.

I laugh too. "That is awful, but you have to expect that from her."

We keep laughing, totally missing Hunter's and Missy's comments. By the time we get control of ourselves, the judges have moved on to a woman named Candace. Candace's color scheme and design style are much more my taste — a cute shift dress done in khakis and browns and subtly accented with red trim.

"She's really good," I whisper.

Missy apparently agrees. "Honey," she says, "you are the reason we have this show. Bravo."

Alex rolls her eyes. "Way to explain why you like her stuff, Missy. Did you have to go to school to come up with that critique?"

The judges finish up with the remaining designers and announce who's safe. In the end, the man with the blue tuxedo and the woman who designed the fluorescent coat are in the bottom two. But before they can announce who will be going home, Barry is back on the screen.

"You'll find out who stays and who goes home after the break," the host says. "And, teens, don't forget what I said earlier in the show. I have an announcement that's sure to blow you away. But you'll have to stay tuned to find out what it is . . . make sure your notebooks are ready so you don't miss any of the details."

"How could I have possibly forgotten? I've had my notebook ready for an hour," I mumble.

Alex frowns. "Jeez, you must really be excited about this announcement. You've been so busy obsessing about the news that you didn't even make your own design today."

I look down at my sketchpad in surprise. Alex is right. Usually, I try to keep up with the challenges by sketching my own versions of what the judges want. But today my sketchpad is totally blank.

The *Design Diva* music suddenly sounds and I quickly look back up at the TV. Barry is standing right where we left him. "And we're back!" he says. "It's never easy to be sent home, but it's especially hard at this point in the competition. And yet, we must say goodbye to one of you." Barry turns to face the designer of the blue tux. "Zack," he says, "the judges have spoken. You, unfortunately, have to put up with them another week. You are safe! Serena, we're sorry to see you go."

I groan. "I hate it when he does that! Poor Serena must have thought she was safe when Barry started his speech."

"The fake-outs are the worst," Alex agrees. "Can't they just tell us the news already? Even I'm getting impatient!"

Finally, while Serena hugs the remaining designers goodbye and dabs at her eyes with a handful of tissues, Barry turns back to the camera.

"I know we've kept you all in suspense," he starts, "but it's finally time for our big announcement! Teens, is your dream to have your designs be seen everywhere? Do you eat, sleep, and dream fashion? If so, this is your chance. You can be on our new show, *Teen Design Diva*. This will be your opportunity to be judged by Jasmine, hang out with Missy, and stare deep into Hunter's baby blues. And the winner will be awarded the ultimate prize — a fashion internship with a top designer in New York City. We'll start holding auditions in two weeks at locations across the country. The final round, if you make it that far, will be held in Salinas, California. Check out our website for more details and to find out if auditions are happening near you."

The show's end credits start to roll, and Alex and I stare at each other, speechless. Salinas? That's less than an hour from where we live! Can this really be happening?

Alex wipes the pizza grease from her fingers and grabs my design notebook. "Move it, Chloe!" she shouts. "You have designs to plan!"

We run upstairs, and I pinch myself. It hurts. It's happening.

Day to Night

SHIRT
DRESS

BUBBLE
SKIRT

teen
**DESIGN
DIVA**

DRAWING TOOLS

CINCHED
WAIST

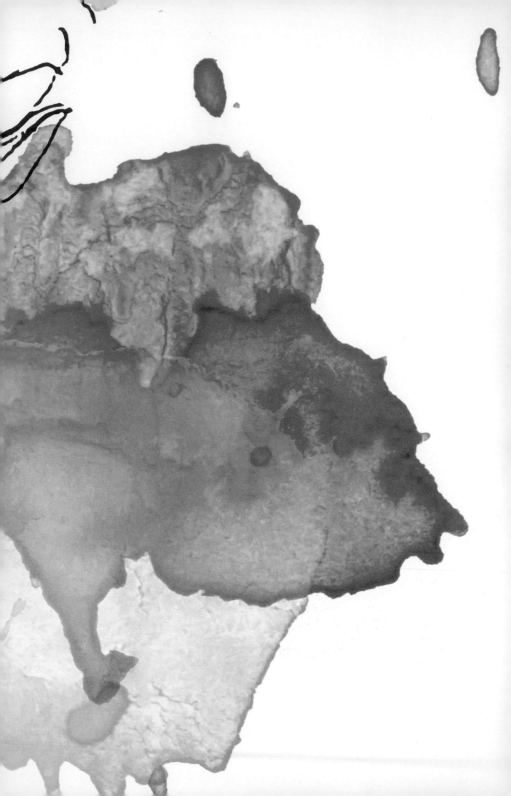

In my room, Alex and I quickly open up my laptop and go to the *Design Diva* website to figure out where the closest auditions will be held. Just like Barry said, the final round will be happening in Salinas at a big rodeo event. (The rest of the world seems to think all of California is like Los Angeles — glossy celebrities everywhere — but the rodeo is huge here in northern Cali.) Salinas is only about forty-five minutes from where I live, so I should be able to convince my parents to let me audition.

The earlier rounds are being held all around the country. Teens from New York to Texas to California will have the chance to compete. It looks like they'll be holding California auditions in two locations — San Francisco and Los Angeles. The first two rounds will narrow it down to forty contestants total, all of whom will gather in Salinas for the final round of auditions. Then the top fifteen designers will get to go to New York to compete and be a part of the show.

I plop down on the floor and pull all my sketchpads out of my desk drawers. Alex drags over the easel, where I've pinned swatches and sample patterns. My room looks like a shrine to all things fashion, and suddenly I'm completely overwhelmed. I have no clue where to start or what to do next.

Thankfully Alex seems to have it all together. She sits back down in front of my laptop, which still has the *Design Diva* website open and ready. "C'mon!" she says. "What are you waiting for?"

I step around my sketches and take a seat on my bed. Just seconds ago I was ready to explode with excitement at the very thought of this opportunity, and now I feel like I'm going to throw up. What's wrong with me?

My fears must be written all over my face because Alex takes one look at me and says, "You know what? Let's just print everything out and go over it step-by-step."

I nod, feeling like an idiot. *Speak!* my brain shouts. "Sounds great!" I say, a little too chipper.

"It'll be better that way anyway," Alex says. She gets the paper from the printer and reads the rules to herself, nodding as she goes. "It looks like pretty simple stuff," she finally says. "The first step of the audition process is to create three original outfits —"

"Three outfits?" I interrupt her. "I can't design three new outfits in two weeks!" My hands are shaking, and I can feel my brain slipping into panic mode.

"Chloe, relax," Alex says. "There's nothing here you can't do. It lays out what the other steps are and—"

I cover my ears and close my eyes to block Alex out. I know I must look like one of my mom's kindergarten students, but I don't care. My floor is covered in all the designs I've ever done — years of energy and dreams. All I've ever wanted is an opportunity like this, and now that it's here I'm acting like a little kid. And I'm too scared to care.

"Okay, I'm going to go," Alex says. She speaks loudly so it's impossible for me to ignore her. "I'll leave these here for you to look over. The rest is up to you."

When I finally open my eyes, Alex is gone. The computer printout of the rules is sitting in her place. I grab the paper and put it on my desk. I'm still not ready to read through the rules quite yet. Best friends have a sixth sense, though, because waiting for me on my desk is a note from Alex. There are only four words on it: "You can do it!"

3

The next morning when I wake up, my head is absolutely throbbing — probably the result of tossing and turning all night long. I don't think I closed my eyes for more than five minutes at a time. What kind of person has the opportunity of a lifetime right in front of them and freaks out? Cowardly Chloe, that's who. Cowardly Chloe. Hmm . . . that sort of has a ring to it. I can just see the label now: two interlocking Cs with a cowering lion in the middle. Ugh. Not what I want my personal logo to be.

With a groan, I force myself to climb out of my cozy bed and walk over to my closet. Choosing an outfit always cheers me up. I study all my shorts, tops, and shoes, looking for something that screams confidence. If I look confident on the outside, maybe it will rub off on the inner me. A girl can hope. I grab a pair of red silk shorts and a long-sleeved, collared blouse, both of which I designed last summer. I pair them with my platform sandals with the cork wedge heel. The bold red seems to do the trick, and by the time I get to school, the cowardly lion has transformed into a scaredey-cat. Progress.

I gather my books at my locker and look around for Alex so I can apologize for being such a spineless weirdo the night before. I don't see her anywhere, but what I do see makes my stomach clench. Walking toward me with her posse of wannabes is Nina LeFleur, my perfectly dressed, number-one rival. Ugh. I can't stand Nina. Not because her outfits rock. Because she's constantly stealing my ideas and pretending they're hers.

It all started when we were five years old. It's hard to imagine that Nina and I actually used to be friends way back then. But one day when she was over at my house, she copied the design for a duct-tape dress I'd made for my Barbie. Then, she told everyone in our neighborhood it was all her idea.

It wouldn't be a big deal if it was just the one time. I mean, we were five, right? But Nina struck again when we were in sixth grade. She saw my patterns for a pink, sparkly top and made her own identical version. And then she wore hers the same day I wore mine. Everyone called us Pinkalicious, like that picture book.

But the absolute worst was when we were freshman. I was creating a dress that I was incredibly proud of for the school fashion show. I worked so hard on it. Guess who else was working on something for the fashion show? Yep, Nina. One day, my patterns just disappeared, and the bobbin on my sewing machine, which supplies the underside of the stitch when you're machine sewing, was gone. Nina's design, which was eerily close to what I had been working on, ended up winning.

Today, like usual, Nina is surrounded by a crowd of groupies. Like Nina, her followers are all blonde. And, like her, their hair color comes straight from a box. Their outfits are nice enough, but something is always just a little off. It's like Nina gave them a handbook detailing what to wear so they would never upstage her. Today, for example, Nina is sporting a sheer violet top over dark skinny jeans, and her five-foot frame gets a boost from high-heeled, metallic sandals. From my spot near my locker, I can hear the wannabes gushing to Nina about how amazing she looks. I want to throw up.

Just then, Alex appears next to me. "Good thing I didn't eat breakfast or I'd be blowing chunks right now," she mutters.

I laugh. Alex always knows what to say. "I can't stand her," I mutter.

SEQUINS

SEQUINS

Gathered and girly!

DOODLES AND *Ideas*

Simple shoes

Simple shoes

Bo...
con...

short

Cowardly
CHLOE

"Who can?" Alex replies. "She's awful."

I gesture toward the groupies. "Well, they clearly don't think so."

Alex rolls her eyes in response. "She has them brainwashed."

"They'd worship me, you know, if she didn't steal all my designs," I complain.

Alex sucks in her breath. She does this when she's annoyed, and I know I'm probably the one she's annoyed with right now. I do whine about Nina — a lot. But sometimes I just can't help it! She deserves it.

"Sorry," I mumble apologetically. "I know I complain about her a lot."

Alex shakes her head. "It's not that you complain about her. You have every right to. In fact, if I were you, I wouldn't have taken the high road so many times." She pauses. "It's just that now you finally have a chance to prove you're better, and . . ." Her voice trails off.

"And I'm totally wimping out," I finish for her with a small smile.

"Kind of," Alex agrees.

Just then, Nina spots us down the hallway. She smiles extra big when she sees me, doing her fake Miss America wave, but her eyes are anything but nice. "Hey, hon!" she calls. "Looove the top!"

"Thanks!" I say back, giving her a tense smile.

"Why does she insist on acting like you're friends?" Alex asks. "Everyone knows you guys can't stand each other."

I shrug. "Who knows. I just figure it's easier to go along with it." I watch as Nina and her followers turn a corner and disappear. Alex is right. Do I always want to fake smile and think about what could have been? Or do I want to do something?

Do something, I decide. I turn to face Alex. "After school. You. Me. Mimi's."

Alex's face lights up. "Well, thank goodness for Nina. Maybe having her around isn't all bad after all."

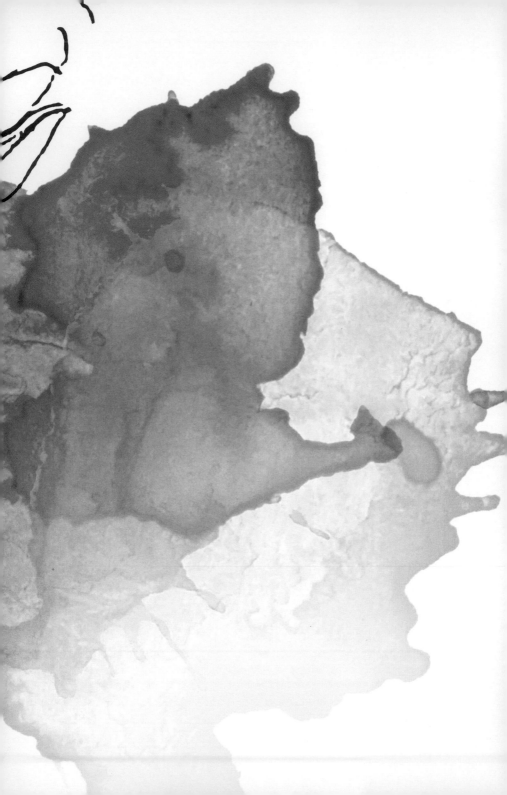

As soon as Alex and I are done for the day, we head to Mimi's Thrifty Threads. If you ask me, Mimi's is basically the best store in all of Santa Cruz. Picture Willy Wonka's Chocolate Factory and then replace all the candy with every piece of fabric, strand of beading, and spool of thread imaginable, and you've got Mimi's. Whenever I enter that store, it's like Christmas and my birthday all rolled into one. And the best part is Mimi.

"Girls!" Mimi squeals when she sees us enter the store. She runs over and pulls us both into a big hug, her standard greeting.

"Love the hat, Meems," Alex says, eyeing Mimi's newest creation — a straw hat with a plastic bird perched on top of it.

"Thanks, darling," Mimi says, reaching up to adjust her hat. "I was thinking of adding an egg for the bird to sit on, but I thought that might be overdoing it. What do you think?"

I smile. "Maybe just a little." But the thing is, even if there was an egg perched up there, Mimi could carry it off. Her styles would look completely insane on anyone else, but they totally work for her.

"You're probably right," Mimi says, but I can tell she's a little disappointed. "Anyway, what brings my favorite girls in today?" Helping with designs and sketches always perks Mimi up. And despite her eccentric style, she has a great eye when it comes to figuring out what others need. Years ago, she even designed clothes for huge Hollywood productions.

Alex points at me. "Chloé is going to try out for that new show: *Teen Design Diva*."

Mimi claps her hands together in delight. "Really? Well, that's just fabulous! How can I help?"

"Well, I didn't even read the requirements yet," I admit, blushing a little. "I guess I should do that first."

"I read them," Alex says. "For the first round of auditions you're supposed to create three outfits that speak to your fashion sense — whatever that means."

"That's a cinch," says Mimi. "That just means clothing that represents who Chloe is and what she'd wear. Easy."

MIMI'S NEW CREATION!

STRAW HAT

PLASTIC BIRD

OTHER HAT IDEAS

FABRIC BOLTS

Mimi's THRIFTY THREADS

✓ Thread
✓ Fabric
✓ Accents

I let Mimi and Alex chat about me like I'm not even there while I start thinking about what clothing screams *Chloe*. Definitely not the red shorts I wore today. Sure, they look good, but the red is much louder than my usual style. And they look much more confident than I'm feeling lately.

As if to prove my point, the chimes on the door ring, and Nina walks in with two mini-Ninas in tow. She gives me a big, fake smile when she sees me. "Chloe!" she says, voice syrupy sweet. "I should have known you'd be here."

I just stare at her. "Yep," I finally say. Brilliant, Chloe. Just brilliant.

"Let me guess," Nina says. "You're trying out for *Teen Design Diva* too, right?" She's still smiling, but her eyes have narrowed, like I'm a dartboard and she's getting ready to shoot.

Too? I think to myself. Of course. I should have known Nina would be auditioning. That means I'll have to compete against her. Again. This day just got about a thousand times worse.

Alex opens her mouth to say something, but I beat her to the punch. "Yep," I say again. Way to use your words, Chloe.

Nina laughs and elbows the mini-Ninas, both of whom laugh too. "I'm sure you'll do great!" she says, all fake sincerity. "Maybe you can practice some designs on your Barbies. Do you still do that?"

I'm standing there speechless, but Alex looks ready to explode. "Listen up, Nasty — I mean Nina. If you went head to head, Chloe would wipe the floor with you. Hands down. Assuming you don't cheat, of course. But that's pretty much impossible for you, isn't it?"

Now it's Nina's turn for silence.

Mimi takes advantage of the moment to speak up. "That's enough, ladies," she says. "This store is a place of creativity and peace and not put-downs."

"Sorry," Alex mumbles quietly. But it's clear she's not sorry at all.

"I was just making friendly conversation," Nina says with a fake pout. "I can't help it if they took it the wrong way. Come on, girls, we'll come back later." She and her groupies turn and leave the store before any of us can respond.

I think back to what Mimi said about the first challenge. *Easy peasy.*

Maybe for someone like Nina. Someone willing to do anything to get ahead. Maybe I need to be fiercer and meaner, but Cheating Chloe is not who I am.

I look out the window of Mimi's store and see Nina and her followers in the distance. They're only specks now . . . so why am I still so intimidated?

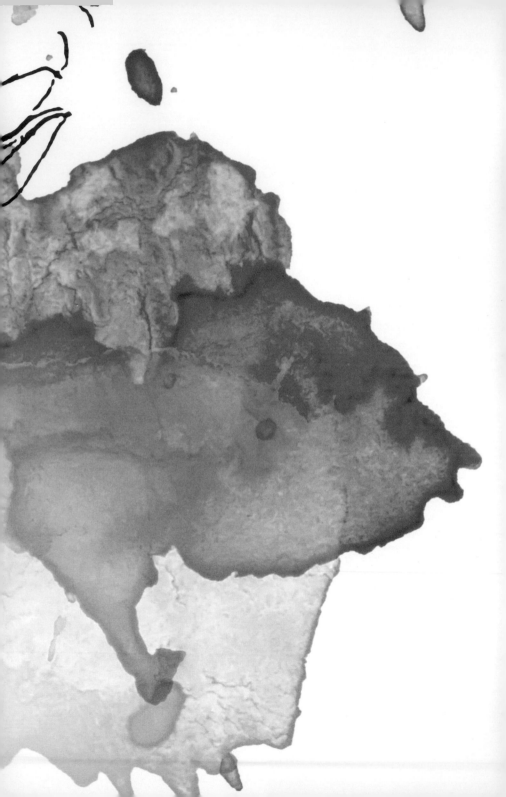

5

When I'm safely back in my room later that evening, I try to put the competition out of my mind, but it's not easy. My sketchpads are sitting right where Alex left them. My desk is covered with fabric swatches, tracing paper, colored pencils, and croquis — quick figure sketches — showcasing my latest designs. Even my walls serve as a canvas for sample fashion ideas. This is all I've ever wanted, but now everything I've done seems too simple and amateur. I have no idea what Nina has planned, but I'm sure her clothing will scream sophistication.

Well, sophistication and snobbery.

I curl up in a ball on my bed and try to resist the urge to cry. I hate feeling sorry for myself, but sometimes it feels good to wallow. For some reason it's not as scary as imagining what can or can't happen. I don't know how long I lie there, but eventually a knock on my door forces me to take a break from my sniffling.

"Chloe," says my mom softly, "can I come in?"

I sit up and see her standing in the doorway. She's holding a large blue binder I haven't looked at in months, not since my gramps died.

The binder is a collection of every clipping ever written about Gramps's rodeo days. When he was younger, he used to ride broncos and later became a rodeo clown, or bullfighter as they're called now. He was quick and strong, and the bull riders depended on him to distract the bull. Gramps was one of the best in his field and loved his job despite the danger. After he retired, he still went to the rodeos and found ways to help. When he died last year, more than a hundred cowboys and riders came to the funeral. I miss him every day — and seeing the blue binder brings it all rushing back.

I motion for my mom to come in, and I wipe away my tears with the back of my hand. Mom takes a seat beside me on the bed and brushes my hair out of my eyes. Without asking why I'm crying, she opens the album.

"This picture here," Mom says, pointing to one of Gramps when he was in his twenties, "is when your gramps first started out. The bullfighters were dressed as clowns back then. A lot of the time, they didn't get the respect they deserved, but Gramps loved it anyway. He was determined to prove he was more than entertainment."

Mom flips through the pages, and I see Gramps at different shows, wearing different colored uniforms. In every picture, he's smiling and his eyes are filled with excitement. Mom flips more pages to a ceremony where Gramps received an award for best rodeo clown. Another picture shows him older and wearing the same uniform as the riders. His face looks so proud. We flip through more photos of Gramps standing with his buddies and others where he's retired and one of the noted speakers at the Cowboys and Chocolate Festival.

"If he could see me now, he'd think I was a wimp," I say. "Gramps never let anything get him down."

My mother shakes her head. "No, he wouldn't, and that's not why I showed this to you. But he would tell you to believe in yourself. He'd also tell you to lean on your family and friends if you need help. Like Alex." Mom smiles.

I sigh. My mom must have talked to Alex. That's how she knew I was upset. "She has enough confidence for both of us," I say.

"Then what's the problem?" my mom asks. "Why don't you?"

I take a deep breath. "Nina," I say. "She's trying out for this new show too." There's no need to explain more. My mom knows all about that history.

Mom nods. "Okay, I get that you might be a little worried about that, but you're you and Nina's Nina. So, she didn't play fair before. It doesn't matter. If you make your best designs, that's all that counts."

Mom smiles warmly and kisses the top of my forehead before standing up. She leaves the binder on my bed and walks over to my desk to study my templates and the sketchpad on my floor. "These are great, honey. I can see range you didn't have before." She holds up a sketch of an ombré skirt I did recently — the color starts out pink at the top then fades to white and finally to black at the bottom. "This skirt, for example. It stays with your style but brings in some subtle hints of color."

I get off my bed and walk over to my mom. I look at the designs in her hands and see them with clear eyes. She's right; my range has grown. Even if the red shorts I'm wearing today didn't make me as confident as I'd hoped, I wouldn't have dared to wear such a bright color years ago.

"Why don't you take a look at the contest rules?" says Mom. "Let me know how I can help."

"Thanks, Mom," I say, giving her a hug.

Mom hugs me tightly. "You know," she says with a little laugh, "when your dad and I first heard about this contest, we had a long talk about whether or not we should let you do it. Not that we're concerned about driving to and from San Francisco for auditions. That's not a big deal. But if you make it through all three rounds, it'll mean a few weeks in New York City. The competition could be a lot of pressure. But we know this is your dream, so we decided we would let you. I'll have the summer off from teaching and could go with you, so that would make it better. But you never even came to ask us. Who would have thought *I'd* be the one to have to convince *you*."

I laugh. I wouldn't have thought that's how things would end up either. "I guess I should thank Alex too."

"Good idea," says Mom. She gives me another quick hug before she leaves.

I sit on my bed and begin to read the contest info that Alex printed out. When I finish, I take a deep breath and let it out slowly. I wait for the clammy hands, the quick beating of my heart, and the nervous feeling in my stomach. But to my surprise, none of them come.

Alex was right. There's nothing here I can't do. I take this as my cue and run out the door back to Mimi's. I have three outfits to plan!

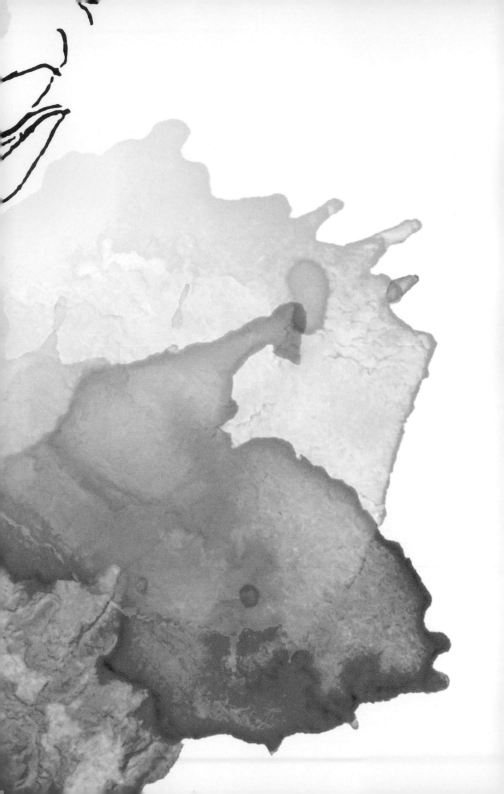

6

I rush through Mimi's door so quickly that I send fabric swatches flying to the floor.

"Oh, shoot! Sorry!" I say, bending down to pick up all the pieces I've managed to make a mess of. When I finally get up, I expect Mimi to look shocked by my crazy behavior, but instead she's smiling. I brush my messy hair back with my fingers. "Never know what you're going to get with me, huh?" I say, smiling back sheepishly.

"I just see a very excited girl," says Mimi. "Besides, you don't need to explain anything to me, honey. Just tell me what has you so hyper!"

"Thanks, Mimi," I say. I can always count on her. "So, I finally read all the info about the competition. They're holding the first couple rounds of auditions all over the country, and then they'll narrow it down. For the first challenge, I have to design and create three different outfits and present them to the judges. The second round is supposed to focus on accessories. The rules said something about showing our creativity and versatility as designers. Then, there's a third round where they'll bring everyone together in Salinas and narrow it down to fifteen designers. That's who gets to go to New York. But I don't know what the challenge will be. They must only give you details if you make it that far."

Mimi holds up a hand to stop me. "No, honey, not *if* you make it that far. *When* you do. Because I know you will." She pats my hand encouragingly.

I beam. "Okay, *when* I make it that far," I correct myself. It feels weird saying that, like I'm going to jinx the whole thing if I let myself believe it. "And after that there's a final round that determines the top ten. One month in New York! Can you believe it?"

Mimi sighs wistfully. "Oh, I loved living there. It's one of the fashion capitals of the world," she says. She stares off into the distance, then shifts her attention back to the present. "Ah, but that was a long time ago. I'm too old to live that hectic lifestyle now." She laughs and shakes her head, obviously remembering something crazy from her past. Young Mimi must have been one heck of a character. "However, you, my dear, are in for something amazing. I can just picture you there. You'll fit right in."

I grin with excitement. I can totally see it. The glitz, glamour, lights. The loud, big-city life. All things I've read about and seen on television. Suddenly, I see myself blending in, just like Mimi predicted. "I hope so," I say. "It will be nuts, though. We'll be doing a challenge or two a day!"

"I wouldn't worry," says Mimi in a calm, soothing voice. "You can pull it off. Now let's get to work. What's your vision for the first challenge?"

"Well, I'm supposed to create outfits that reflect my own personal style, so I want to create clothes that are clean and classic, but still modern and stylish. Probably minimal print if any. I don't want to use fabric that's too loud or crazy. That's just not me. Maybe something with a subtle print would work, or some cool texture. I need something to make them stand out and set them apart." I realize all of it sounds a bit vague, but Mimi is nodding like she totally gets it.

"That makes perfect sense. If the clothes are supposed to explain your style, you don't want embellishments distracting the judges from the basics. You want your natural talent to shine through," says Mimi.

"Yes, exactly! So maybe tightly woven cotton, some non-stretchy, cotton-poly blends. What else do you think?" I ask. I start walking around the store and feeling the different fabrics Mimi has hanging on bolts on the wall. I start grabbing different materials — some linens, funky faux leather, slippery silk, and cotton blends in neutral shades. I can feel my body buzzing with excited energy as I start to plan my designs and collect fabrics I think will work.

By the time I'm done, my arms are totally full and starting to ache. Carrying all that fabric is a serious workout! I dump the pile of fabrics on the front counter, then gravitate toward a rack of gently used clothing to see if any of it can be cut up and incorporated into my designs. I don't see anything on the rack for my first-round designs, but I decide to treat myself to a sheer, ivory blouse with ruffles down the front that will be the perfect addition to my wardrobe. It's a great neutral, and I can already picture pairing it with this embellished skirt design I've been working on.

When I finally make it to the front counter, it's nothing but a pile of fabric. I didn't realize how much I'd grabbed. The counter must be under that pile somewhere. I see Mimi placing a few more items on the counter too and examine what she's found.

"These are perfect, Mimi. Thanks," I say. I reach out and feel the fabric on top of the pile. "You even found some wool. Nice!"

"We don't have much use for it here in California," Mimi says, "but it's a must in colder locations. Even if you don't use it this round, it might come in handy for something later down the line."

Mimi folds all my fabrics and places them in a neat pile. "Silk?" she says, holding up one of the pieces I grabbed.

Mimi's reaction makes me second-guess my choice a little. I was hesitant about the silk when I picked it up. Silks are really hard to work with. They're shiny and slippery and tough to manage. In fact, I've only attempted one other design with silk before — a black skirt — and it was beyond hideous. I ended up taking it apart and telling my mom to use it as a tablecloth.

"I know it's a risk," I say, "but it's so smooth and soft. I just couldn't resist. Besides, I thought if I could show the judges that I'm willing to take risks with my designs, it might work in my favor."

"Maybe you're right," says Mimi, but I can tell she's not completely sold. "Just don't be a hero with it. I'd stick to the simple running stitch so you can take it apart easily if you need to."

"Thanks, Mimi," I say, giving her a hug. The thank you is for way more than just her sewing advice — it's also for how helpful and encouraging she always is. No matter what.

"No problem, honey," she says as she finishes bagging up my fabrics and the blouse I grabbed. "Let me know if you need anything else."

I pull out my wallet to pay for everything, but Mimi motions for me to put it away. "Today is on me," she says. "Consider it a reward for not giving up."

My mouth drops open in surprise. "No, Mimi, you can't," I say, shaking my head. "It's too much."

"It's my store, and I'll tell you what's too much," Mimi says. "You just go make me proud."

"There has to be something I can do if you won't let me pay," I insist.

Mimi thinks for a minute. "How about this? When you win, make sure you mention Mimi's Thrifty Threads, okay? We'll call it even." She winks at me.

I can't help but smile at Mimi's confidence. I can only hope some of that will rub off on me. "Deal," I say. "And don't worry. When I'm done, you'll have lines out the door."

Mimi's THRIFTY THREADS

RUFFLE BLOUSE TO REINVENT

SPARKLY ACCESSORIES

DESIGN SUPPLIES

Neutrals, Black & White, Sparkles

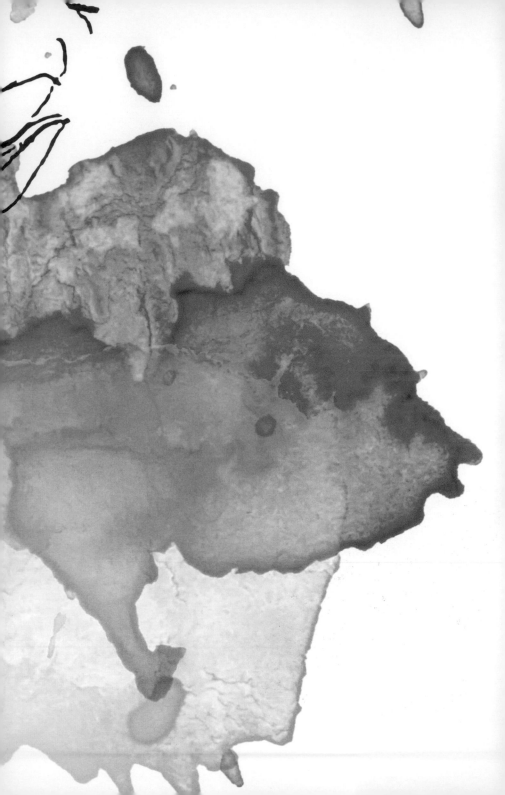

7

A week later, Alex and I are back in my bedroom and hard at work. "What's next, CC?" Alex asks. She's been calling me that ever since I took the plunge and decided to try out for *Teen Design Diva*. She says it stands for Courageous Chloe. Better than Cowardly Chloe, so I'll go with it.

I glance up from where I'm sprawled on the floor and look around the room. The floor is covered with supplies for matching patterns, cutting stencils, and pinning designs. The first round of the competition is next week, and so far I only have one design fully completed. I'm halfway done with the second, but every minute counts, which is why Alex is there helping. Lucky for me, this week is spring break. While everyone else is busy having fun at the beach, Alex and I are busy designing nonstop.

Well, I'm designing, and Alex is offering me words of wisdom and encouragement. At this point, I need them pretty desperately.

Right now, Alex has scissors in one hand and pins in the other. She looks tired, and I feel guilty. This isn't her project. She should be enjoying her spring break and downing milkshakes and burgers at the beach with everyone else, not trapped in my room. "Take a break," I say. "You've been helping me for four hours."

"I can do more if you need me to," Alex says as her stomach growls loudly.

I laugh. "No, your stomach speaks. It demands to be fed. Take a break and go get something to eat. You've done more than enough."

Alex starts to shake her head no just as her stomach lets out another loud protest. She laughs and lets out a defeated sigh. "Just a short break," she agrees, setting down the pins and scissors. "I promise you won't even have the chance to miss me."

I laugh again and wave her out the door. "Take your time. Eat some salt-and-vinegar fries, okay?" I feel my own stomach rumbling, but I ignore it. Designing is more important that eating at this point.

"You got it, CC," says Alex as she dashes out the door. A minute later I hear the front door slam, and she's gone.

The truth is, while I've been super grateful to have Alex's help so far, I need some time alone with my designs. I need to know I'll be able to think through ideas and problems on my own without having Alex there to bail me out if my brain freezes. After all, if — no, *when*, as I have to keep reminding myself — I make it to New York, Alex won't be able to come with me. I need to live up to my new CC nickname — the one where I wear a superhero cape and save outfits from ruin with a single stitch.

I look at my first completed design, which is hanging on the outside of my closet door. It's a white dress with a fitted bodice and a full, gathered skirt. The color and material make the piece casual enough for school, especially if it's paired with tights and flats, but it's also something you could throw on for a last-minute party and jazz up with a cute blazer and some jewelry.

I decided to tackle the silk dress next since I was on a roll, but things did *not* go as well as I'd hoped. Silk is really hard to work with, just like Mimi said. I knew she had a point, but I was hoping I'd have better luck this time around than I've had in the past. But silk is so slippery that it's hard to manipulate. Even though I used the simple running stitch that Mimi suggested, the fabric refused to cooperate — it kept bunching up. I finally decided to take a break because I was getting so

CONTRASTING INSERTS AT
SHOULDERS & WAIST

FULL
SKIRT

REMOVABLE
COLLAR
&
OPTIONAL BELT

COURAGEOUS
CHLOE

CROQUIS
AND
Notes

frustrated. I'll come back to that piece when I'm feeling more confident.

The design I'm working on now is hanging half-made on one of the many mannequins Mimi gave me years ago. I've had tons of patterns and creations draped on it over the years, but the ones I'm working on for my audition are more important than all the rest. After studying my first dress again, which turned out as well as I'd imagined, I'm starting to second-guess this next design. I know if Alex were still around, she'd probably say, "You've already second-, third-, and fourth-guessed it. Just go with it."

Okay, I think to myself, *I'm going with it.* So far, I have a pair of leather-trimmed leggings draped across the mannequin. The faux leather accents along the vertical side seams make them look like a modern tuxedo pant. I study the pattern I've sketched for a slim-fitting tunic to pair with the leggings, and something finally clicks in my brain.

Turning, I paw through the pile of fabric from Mimi's until I find what I'm looking for — the remaining fabric scraps from the faux leather I bought. By itself the tunic looks a little too plain and simple, but adding leather panels to the shoulders will give it a tough edge and tie it together with the leggings.

I grin as I hold the fabric up to my dress form. Alex is always telling me I think too much. If I'd just let myself relax, everything would come together easier. She's right, but my brain doesn't always work that way. Now, however, it's on a roll. I pin the white fabric for the tunic to the mannequin's chest and hold up the leather panels at the shoulders. The contrast between the color and textures is perfect, and paired with the tuxedo leggings it's a stylish, sophisticated outfit.

"Yes!" I shout to the empty room. Perfection.

My stomach growls in response, and this time I don't think twice about taking a break. I head to the kitchen and make myself a sandwich, scarfing it down quickly. When I'm done eating, I decide to run to Mimi's and give her an update on my designs.

I'm still riding high on the excitement of my second design coming together when I burst through Mimi's door. Her face lights up when she sees me. "That smile must have a great story to tell," Mimi says.

"It does!" I agree. "I came up with the perfect idea for my second design!" I launch into an explanation of my fabric choice, and Mimi's face suddenly falls. "You don't think it will work?" I ask.

"No, hon, it's not that—" Mimi starts to say, but I cut her off.

Studded
Trim

TUNIC TOP IDEAS

"Simple
Chic"

2ND LOOK DEVELOPMENT *Sketches*

leather TRIM

Lar chec boo

Leather SHOULDERS

Add chain belt?

Leather strip on side

Tuxedo Jegging?

silk with l cu pa

SKINNY PANTS

LEATHER ACCENTS

Neutrals, Black & White

"I know the black and white sounds a little stark, but the texture of the leather and the softer fabric play off each other really well," I say.

Mimi's face still looks panicked, and I don't know what to do — she is normally so supportive and encouraging. Maybe I'm not doing a very good job explaining my design.

"Chloe, let's talk about this later," Mimi says quietly, nodding pointedly toward the back of the store.

"Wh—" I start to say. But just then Nina walks out of the back room, and I immediately understand why Mimi didn't want to talk. In all my excitement, I didn't even hear Nina come in. She probably snuck into the store on purpose, ready to spy, when she noticed me going in. I bet she heard me talking about my design, and Mimi noticed her too late to do anything.

"Chloe!" says Nina, all fake cheer and excitement. "Imagine running into you here! I feel like I haven't seen you in forever. What have you been up to?"

"Oh, just busy creating," I say, my own plastic smile firmly in place. I don't want her to know she's rattled me. "You know how that is, I'm sure."

"Oh, totally," Nina says, smirking at me. "In fact, I should probably get going. I just got a few amazing ideas, and I have to start sketching right away. Wouldn't want to forget them. Toodles!" She blows me an air kiss, which makes me want to gag, and then bounces out the door.

As soon as Nina disappears, so does my smile. I put my head in my hands and groan.

"I'm sorry, sweetheart," Mimi says, patting my back. "I tried to warn you."

I shake my head. "It's not your fault," I say. "Just the story of my life."

I see Mimi trying not to smile at my melodramatic reaction. I force myself to pull my head out of my hands and stand up. "I guess I should get going too," I say. "Might as well get started on my other ideas."

Unlike Nina, I don't skip home. Instead, I drag my feet and take my time. Suddenly I'm not nearly as excited or ready to confront the designs I was so pumped up about only an hour ago.

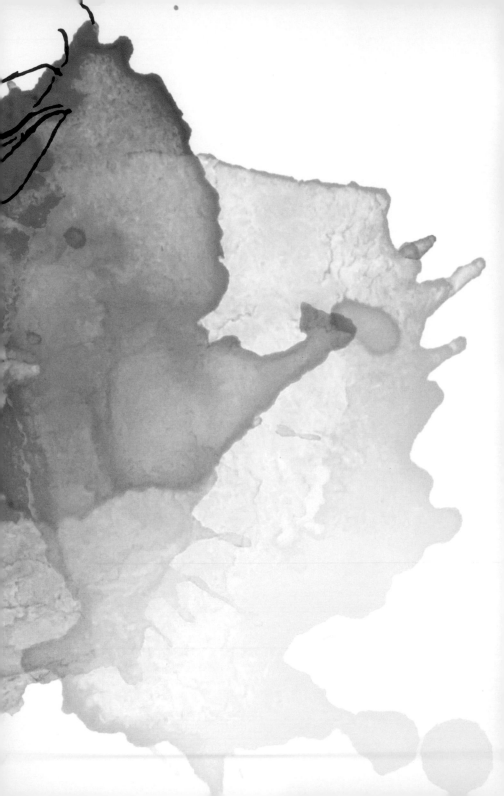

8

When I get home, I plop myself down at the kitchen table beside my mom. She's reading the paper but sets it aside when she sees me. "Cookie?" she offers, holding out the plate.

I'm too bummed to eat and shake my head no, but my hands seem to have a mind of their own. They grab an Oreo and shove it in my mouth. My mom gets up to pour me a glass of milk, and then sits back down to wait for me to tell her what's wrong.

After a few minutes, I take a deep breath. I'm feeling slightly better. Whether you're six or sixteen, cookies, milk, and moms make everything better. When I'm done chewing, I say only one word. "Nina."

Mom nods. "I figured it might be something like that," she says. "You know what, though? I've been dying to hear all about your designs. I've been trying to stop myself from peeking before you got home. Can you show them to me while we talk?"

I clean the crumbs off my hands. "Sure, let's go upstairs," I agree.

My mom follows me up to my room. "So, you want me to just tell you about them?" I ask.

My mom nods like an excited kid and sits down on my bed.

I walk to my closet door, where my first design is hanging, and pretend my mom is one of the *Design Diva* judges. "What you see here is my take on a bubble dress," I say, trying to sound confident and in charge. "I chose this lightweight material because the color and weight of the fabric make it easy to dress up or down. The fitted bodice and natural waist are flattering on most body types, and the full skirt helps provide contrast and proportion."

"Can I come look at it?" Mom asks.

"Sure," I reply. While she comes over to inspect the material and shape of the dress, I unearth a pair of metallic silver flats I'd just about given up on. They'd been buried deep in the back of my closet, but it turns out they were just waiting for this dress to make their debut.

My mom walks over to the mannequin displaying my second design, which is still a work in progress, and I let her view the outfit from various angles before saying anything myself. "This one is fun," she finally says. "It can work with flats or heels, right?"

"Definitely," I say.

My mom is by no means a major fashionista, but she and I have talked so much fashion over the years that she's started to look at fashion magazines without my prompting. She even bought *GQ* for my dad so he can get in on the "family hobby," as she calls it.

Mom studies the fabric I'm using for the tunic more closely. "I'm really interested in your choice of colors here," she says. "This is a very monochromatic palette. Can you tell me more about it?"

I can tell my mom is trying to play the part of judge, asking a question she's heard Missy ask dozens of times on *Design Diva*. "I'm glad you brought that up," I say, grinning. "I've been reading a lot recently about monochromatic styles being popular, which is why I chose to stick with black and white. The contrast between the colors is very edgy, especially with the leather detailing on the leggings and shoulders. Some chunky metallic jewelry will add shine to the outfit and still keep the palette refined and simple."

By the time I finish explaining my vision for the design, I'm just as happy and excited as I was when it first came to me. Suddenly it hits me. "Nina doesn't matter," I say. "I came home all mad and dejected about her stealing another idea, but it doesn't matter what she does, does it?"

Mom gives me an encouraging smile. It's clear she realized this long before I did. "Not when it comes to you, it doesn't," she tells me. "You have to remember that there are always going to be people going after the same thing you are. Some will play fairly, and others won't. But in the end, it's how you handle yourself and what *you* do that matters. You have beautiful designs; you always have. Sure, to an untrained eye some designs may look the same. But that's how it is in the fashion world. To those who get it, your uniqueness will shine through."

I want to smack myself for not coming to this realization sooner, but I guess everything happens in its own time for a reason. "Maybe having Nina there actually helped push me forward," I say.

My mom scrunches up her nose. "Let's not give her *too* much credit," she says with a laugh. "But I guess in some ways she has."

I clap my hands together, excited to move forward and finish the rest of my designs. "I'll just have to motivate myself from now on," I say.

Mom smiles. "That's the spirit."

"Do you want to keep me company while I work on my next piece?" I ask. This final design will take the most time. It's my silk idea, and I have to pay it a lot of attention, but I also know I could use someone to stop me from getting too serious.

"I thought you'd never ask!" Mom says. "Talk me through it." She takes a seat beside me on the floor, and I spread my sketches out in front of us.

My mom and I spend the rest of the day talking, laughing, pinning, and sewing. When Alex calls to check in, we tell her we have it under control. By the end of the week, I'm ready and confident. Judges, here I come.

SOFT & FLOWY DETAIL?

Fabric Details at Waist and Neckline?

3RD LOOK DEVELOPMENT Sketches

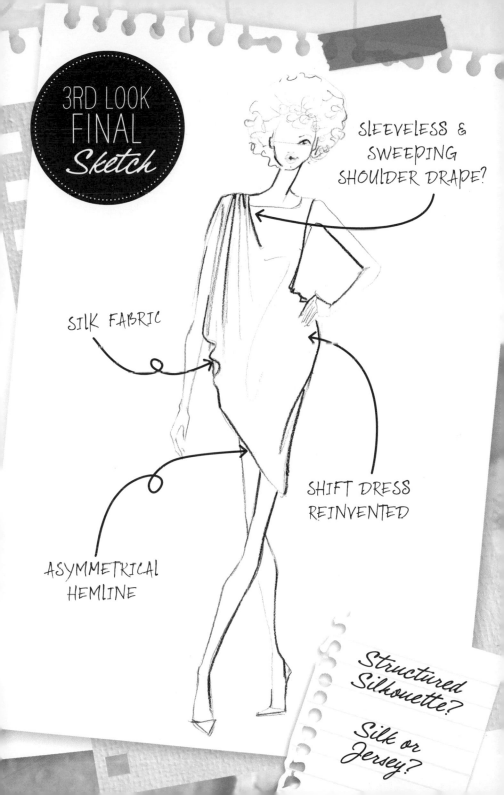

9

I glance up at the clock in the hallway and watch as the second hand moves slowly around the face. Even though I can see the clock's hands moving, it feels like time is standing still. It's finally the day of *Teen Design Diva* auditions, and we've been waiting since seven o'clock this morning. I couldn't sleep anyway, so my mom eventually agreed to get on the road to San Francisco early.

Thank goodness we got here when we did. Even though we arrived early, I'm still number twenty on the list. An hour after we arrived, the count was already past one hundred, and the producer said anyone else would have to wait until at least the next day if not later. Apparently they can't guarantee everyone will even get a chance to audition.

It's almost eleven o'clock now, and they're on number nineteen. Finally.

Alex lets out a big yawn, which makes my mom and me yawn too. It seems to be contagious since everyone around us is yawning. "How much longer?" Alex asks sleepily. Her eyes are starting to drift closed.

"I'm next," I reply. I'm ready to go, but I'm also starting to get nervous as my time draws closer.

Just then, the producer appears with her clipboard and searches the list of numbers. "Number twenty!" she calls. "Chloe Montgomery?"

I leap up. "Right here."

My mom stands up and gives me a big hug. "Go get 'em," she says. "And remember that no matter what happens, your dad and I are so proud of you."

Alex jumps up too and squeezes me tight. "You've got this in the bag, CC," she whispers to me. "Knock those judges dead."

I carefully gather my designs and make my way to the auditorium where the judges are waiting. My palms are sweating, and I have to remind myself to stay calm as I walk up the steps to the stage. I hang my designs on the rack beside me and turn to face the judges.

I almost can't believe it. It's really them! Jasmine looks back at me with her mouth set in a stern line. Missy is all teeth and smiles. And Hunter — how did I never notice that adorable dimple in his left cheek?

I must stare at them a bit too long because I hear Jasmine clear her throat. "Girl," she says, "we haven't got all day. You have something you want to tell us about?"

I snap to attention and become the professional me I practiced in front of the mirror, my parents, and Alex. I start with my first dress. "For this dress, I wanted something that could transition easily from a daytime look to an evening look," I explain. "It's important for me to have something I can wear to school and also out later with friends. And because I tend to keep my style simple, I wanted something that reflected that. That's why I opted for this neutral fabric. The color can be dressed up or down with accessories depending on when and where it's being worn, which makes the dress extremely versatile."

I catch sight of Hunter's face as I'm talking the judges through my design, and he looks impressed. Or at least I think he does. My confidence builds as I get to my next design — the monochromatic leggings and tunic.

"I really liked the idea of using two very different colors and fabrics for this outfit in order to create contrast," I explain. "The subtle leather accents at the shoulders and along the side seams of the leggings

Fitted
Bodice

Full
Gathered
Skirt

1ST LOOK
FINAL
Sketches

Pair
with
Metallic
heels!

1ST LOOK FINAL *Design*

SLEEVELESS BODICE

CINCHED WAIST

FULL SKIRT

POP OF COLOR OR METALLIC

add some visual interest without being too loud or overwhelming, which again, sticks to my personal style aesthetic — simple but chic."

I see Jasmine crack a small smile of approval at my explanation.

"Lovely," says Missy when I've finished describing my first two pieces. "So far I'm in your corner. Tell us about your final design, Chloe."

This is it, I think to myself. *If you pull this off, you've made it through the first round.* My throat has suddenly gone dry, and I swallow hard. Hunter and Missy are still smiling at me, but I see Hunter glance at his watch. Jasmine's face is clearly impatient.

"So, um, for this piece I chose silk?" I hate how my voice goes up at the end, like I'm asking a question. *Be confident, Chloe. Come on,* I think.

I take a deep breath and keep going. "To be honest, I haven't done much work with silk before," I confess, "but I wanted to challenge myself."

Was it smart or dumb to be so up front about not having much experience with silk? Oh, well. Too late to take it back now. Just keep going. "But since I didn't want to fall completely on my face, I decided to create a simpler dress pattern and went with a shift," I say. "I added an asymmetrical hem and sweeping shoulder drape to create some visual interest and add a more modern twist."

I pause to see if the judges have anything to say, but they're still staring at me expectantly. "Right, so one of the best things about shift dresses is their versatility. They look simple, but they work with any body type. Add a belt, and you get more definition around the waist. Wear it loose, and you can share it with a friend who's a different size."

"Do you mind if I come take a look at the stitching?" Jasmine asks.

"Sure. Missy and Hunter, do you want to come look too?" I suggest, getting bold.

Missy and Hunter laugh. "Why not?" Hunter says.

The three of them walk around my shift dress, examining the fabric and stitching. I know what I envisioned for the dress didn't come together, because like Mimi predicted, the silk I chose was super difficult to work with. Even after taking a break from my design and coming back to it, things didn't improve. I managed to pull the dress together, and it's better than what I've done in the past. But still . . . I know it's not great.

I hope the judges don't notice the fraying at the edge of the asymmetrical hem, but I'm sure they do. I should have used my serger to fix them. Why didn't I think of

that before? I'm seriously starting to regret letting them all come up, but thankfully after a few minutes they move toward my first two designs, and I let out a sigh of relief. At least they'll see how careful I was with those.

Finally, the three judges finish their in-depth examination of my work and head back to their table. They say nothing else to me, but lean their heads together and talk amongst themselves. It seems to take forever, and the suspense is killing me. Finally, after a few minutes, they all sit back in their seats and look straight at me.

"I'll go first," Jasmine says, and I mentally brace myself for whatever she has to say. "Let's start with the good. I'm very impressed with your creative vision and clear sense of personal style, which is rare in someone so young. Even if you hadn't told us, I can tell from all your designs that your style is minimalist yet chic, and I like that I didn't have to rack my brain to figure that out. I can't say the same about most of the designs I've seen today. One girl told us her style was 'zombie sweet.' Puh-leeze. That's not a style. It's a Halloween costume."

"Jazz," Hunter interrupts her. "Tone it down. They're kids."

Jasmine lets out an agitated sigh. "Okay, then. I'll try to be nice about what I don't like."

I plaster a smile on my face and will myself not to start crying. *She liked a lot of your designs, just remember that*, I tell myself.

"Sweetie," Jasmine starts, and the word sounds so unnatural from her, "why silk? I mean, it's high school. And it's not a party dress; you're billing it as everyday. Who has the time to clean and take care of silk on a daily basis? It also wrinkles easily. I mean, I can stretch my imagination and give it to you in terms of style, but girlfriend, the stitching. Uh-uh. Not gonna fly."

My smile starts to disappear, and I feel my eyes getting watery. The funny thing is, this is Jasmine being nice, and I know it. If I were a regular adult on her show, she'd really let me have it.

But before the tears can spill over, Hunter jumps in. *Focus on the dimple, focus on the dimple*, I tell myself.

"Chloe, you have real talent," he starts. "That's clear to all three of us. I won't repeat Jasmine's points on personal style, but they're spot on. So, let me get to the one piece that stumped us. I saw where you were going with the silk. And I admire someone who's willing to take a risk, especially in a high-pressure situation like this. I noticed you tried to fix some errors by using the overcast stitch. The problem was that the silk still bunched up. But—"

I must look like I'm about to cry again because Missy interrupts. "Darling, you've got style and we all see it. I mean look at those heels you have on today! I'm obsessed!"

I smile for real this time and try not to laugh. My shoes have absolutely nothing to do with this competition and we all know it, but I can see why they keep Missy around. Without her positive feedback, the stage would be one big sobfest.

Hunter rolls his eyes. "What I was going to say before Missy interrupted me," he says, shooting her an irritated look, "is that those stitching problems can be overcome. Trust me, if anyone saw my first attempts with silk, I'd be fired on the spot. You have potential, kiddo. I'm a yes."

I gasp. He's voting already? And he said yes! I hold my breath and stare at Missy.

"C'mon, darling. You gotta know I'm a yes. Yes, yes, yes!" says Missy.

We all stare at Jasmine, who throws her arms in the air. "Technically, what I say doesn't even matter. You've already got two yesses."

Jasmine is right. What she says doesn't matter in terms of the audition, but to me it matters. A lot. I want to know what she thinks.

Jasmine pauses before continuing. "You're good, Chloe," she finally says. "Really good. Promise me you'll lay off the silk awhile, and it's a definite yes." She grins. I don't think I've ever seen Jasmine grin.

"I promise! I promise!" I rush toward the judges' table and hug all three of them, almost knocking them off their chairs in the process.

Hunter hands me a blue card with instructions for the next leg of the competition, and I rush off the stage and toward the exit. But as I get to the doorway I remember something important — my outfits! As I turn to run back toward the stage, I notice a red blinking light on the ceiling.

Are they taping this part too? I wonder. That's just what I need — me looking like a total ditz on TV. Finally, outfits in hand, I'm out the door again.

My mom and Alex, who is fully awake now, see me with my card in hand and a huge grin on my face and run to meet me. My outfits fall to the ground, and Mom, Alex, and I run and jump in a circle, hugging each other.

"I made it!" I scream.

Alex and Mom both laugh. "Yeah, we sort of got that," Alex says. "What does the card say?"

I glance at the card quickly. "It's instructions for the next round of auditions," I tell them. "I have to make accessories. It says I'm supposed to give one of my designs from this round 'new dimension' and demonstrate my versatility."

Out of the corner of my eye, I see Nina watching us. I figured she had to be around somewhere, but I was too busy being nervous to notice her earlier. She meets my gaze and gives me a thumbs-up. I mouth "thanks" and "good luck" in reply.

"Let's celebrate," says my mom, hugging me tightly. "Chinese food is on me."

The three of us walk out of the building, arms linked. I hold tight to my designs and the note card guaranteeing me entrance to the next round tightly. My brain is already working overtime trying to come up with accessories for the next round of auditions, but I tell it to rest. There's plenty of time to prepare for what's ahead. For now, I'm just going to bask in the moment.

I, Chloe Montgomery, have been criticized by Jasmine DeFabio, taken risks, and made mistakes. Through it all, I didn't crumble. Gramps would be proud.

"So what's next on the fashion star's agenda?" Alex asks as we pile into my mom's car. "Earrings? A necklace? Your adoring fans want to know!"

"I've thought about it very carefully, and I've made a decision. For today, I'm going to keep it simple," I say.

"Bracelet," my mom guesses.

"Better," I reply with a grin. "Lo mein."

We all laugh and drive away, leaving the judges and the first round of auditions behind. For now. Soon, I'll be on that stage again. And I know I'll be ready.

10

Did I say ready? Maybe I spoke too soon. I might be ready for the design portion of this competition, but my newfound celebrity status? Not so much. And that's what Nina and I are now — at least in Santa Cruz. Ever since we made it through the first round of auditions last week, the local papers have been calling nonstop about interviewing us. One newspaper even started a blog called "The Sweethearts of Santa Cruz" so they can keep everyone updated about our progress in the competition.

I'm not sure what they're going to do if Nina and I don't make it to New York City. (Probably start another blog to chronicle our downfall.) Nina clearly isn't bothered by the attention. The way she's acting blowing kisses to anyone within two feet of her — you can tell *not* making it is *not* an option for her.

I wish I had some of Nina's confidence, but there are still two more rounds of auditions to go — accessories and then some mystery rodeo challenge. No one seems to know exactly what the final challenge will entail, especially since the massive California Rodeo, which is held in Salinas, usually isn't held until the third week in July. I heard a rumor that they might be holding a special event to promote *Teen Design Diva* and increase the rodeo hype, but so far it's just that — a rumor.

I guess it makes sense for the local media to milk it for all it's worth now. If Nina and I do end up making it to New York, everything will be taped and kept strictly under wraps. The new set of rules I got is very explicit about keeping everything hush-hush during the show's filming.

"OMG," says Alex in a high-pitched voice as she approaches my locker Friday after school. "Are you Chloe Montgomery? Like for real? Can I get your autograph?"

"Cut it out," I say, blushing. Alex has been getting a huge kick out of my newly minted celeb status. Not only does she get to laugh at my discomfort, but because we're usually joined at the hip, she also gets all the perks without all the embarrassment.

"Aw, come on. You should be enjoying this. Nina sure is," Alex says, nodding down the hallway. Sure enough, I turn and see Nina strutting toward us, fake smile firmly in place. A crowd of mini-Ninas trails behind her.

"Ugh. I can't deal with her right now," I mutter. Nina and I may have called a truce for the time being, but I still don't want to be BFFs. I'm sure she doesn't either, but the reporters who have been hounding us seem to want us to be friends rather than rivals, so she's playing that up for them. I just do my best not to grimace every time she hugs me.

"Chloeee!" Nina squeals as she runs to me. "How have you been, girl?" She leans in and air kisses me on both cheeks.

"Hey, Nina. You ready for the next round?" I ask. The mini-Ninas immediately perk up. They love hearing about anything that has to do with the competition.

"Almost," says Nina, smiling. "There's an art fair tomorrow I'm planning to hit up for inspiration. See you there?"

"Maybe," I say, keeping my answer vague. The truth is, Alex and I have been looking forward to the art fair all week, but I don't need to give Nina any more opportunities to steal my ideas.

"Cool," Nina says with a tight smile. She gives me a quick hug goodbye and motions for her posse to follow. They do, blowing air kisses to me as they go.

"I don't know how you put up with her," Alex says when they're gone. "She's so fake it makes me sick."

"Yeah, tell me about it. But I figure the competition is at least slightly less painful this way." I swing my backpack over my shoulder, and Alex and I head out the school doors. As soon as we're outside, a flash goes off. I shield my eyes and see three reporters, notepads and recorders ready. One of them excitedly motions me over.

I groan and make my way toward the group. Nina is already there, arms moving animatedly as she tells some story.

It seems like my CC nickname is changing again. First it was Cowardly Chloe, then Courageous Chloe. Celebrity Chloe, here I come.

* * *

The next day there's a slight breeze, and the temperature is in the seventies — perfect weather for an art fair. There's nothing worse than looking for bargains under a sweltering sun, while making sure beads of sweat don't ruin the very items you're trying to bargain for. Alex and I have been at the fair for an hour already, and we've barely scratched the surface. That could be because Alex keeps gravitating toward all the food samples. Not that I'm protesting too hard — who turns down free chocolate?

"It's not just the free food that's slowing us down here," says Alex between bites. "Do you even know what you want to design?"

I pretend to be extremely interested in choosing a good chocolate sample so I don't have to answer right away. Alex knows I really have no idea what accessory I want to make yet. I haven't even decided which piece I'm going to accessorize yet. I've managed to narrow it down to the leggings-and-tunic ensemble or the first dress — there's no way I'm revisiting that silk disaster after the judges' comments. I can still hear Jasmine's words: "The stitching. Uh-uh. Not gonna fly."

"Not yet," I finally admit. "I want it to be just right. I'll know it when I see it." I try to sound confident, like that's how designers work. I'm really hoping it's true.

Alex shrugs. "Doesn't matter to me. I could spend all day here. I love people watching, and I see rows and rows of food samples. Just don't try to play it off like it's my fault your hands are empty."

I laugh and give Alex a playful shove. She knows me too well. "If I don't blame you, then I have to blame myself, and that's no fun."

Alex laughs too. "Tough to be you. Ooh, wait. Check out that booth over there," she says. She points across the aisle. "I can't tell exactly what they're selling, but it looks colorful. Come on."

I follow Alex. When it comes to accessories, I tend to be a bit more liberal with color than I am with my wardrobe, which is usually full of neutrals. The right shade of a fiery tone can add spark to a bland top, and a funky metallic can add just enough pop to make an outfit shine.

We arrive at the booth Alex spotted, and for a second I just stand there admiring all the gorgeous jewelry. I browse the pendants on the table. The pieces are all done in shades of orange and red and attached to antique chains. These designs have an old-world feel to them, which is cool, but they won't work with my outfits. The colors aren't right for my leggings and tunic, and the antique feel doesn't match the modern tone of either garment. We walk around more, but nothing on the table is exactly right.

"I need to have some sort of a plan," I tell Alex. "Otherwise I'm never going to be able to pick something. I'm going with the dress." I stare at my best friend expectantly, like she's supposed to jump up and down at the fact that I made a decision.

"Great, let's keep looking," says Alex.

"That's it? No excitement about me finally making a choice?"

Alex laughs. "Oh, sorry. Let me give you the appropriate applause." She pretends her hands are a camera and starts snapping away. People walk around us. Some are amused, and others annoyed that we're in their way.

"Stop," I mumble. Maybe I've gotten too used to the reporters fawning over my design decisions if I expected Alex to pat me on the back.

"Celebrity Chloe," says Alex, transforming her hands into a microphone. "Can you please tell us about how you came to the decision to accessorize the dress?" She holds her faux-microphone up to my mouth.

Some people actually stop, realizing who I am. I want to fall through the ground. "Okay, okay, I get it. No more. Please." I shield my face and walk away from her through the crowd.

Alex runs after me, not ready to let the joke go. I speed up, not watching where I'm going, and end up crashing into a table. When I look up, the boy I see almost makes me forget why I'm there in the first place.

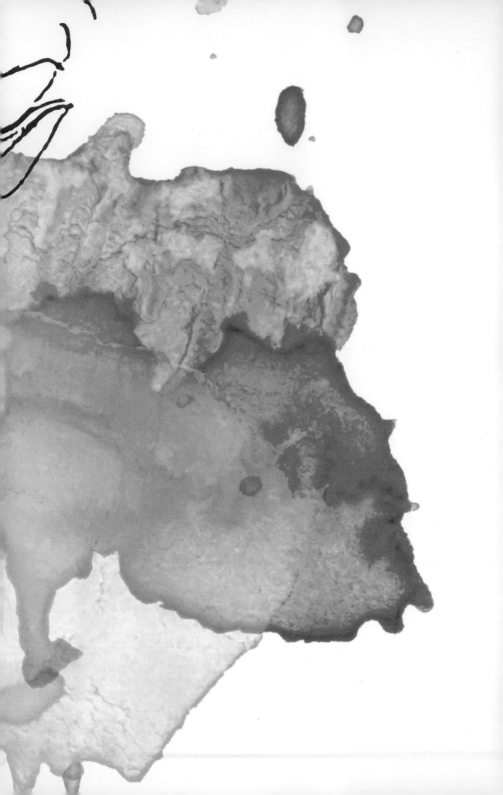

11

"Sorry," I say, gazing into the boy's green eyes. "I wasn't looking where I was going."

The mystery boy smiles at me, and when he does, I see he has a dimple in each cheek. "No harm done," he says, but I can see him rearranging a few of the pieces on the table. "Looked like you were a girl on a mission."

"She definitely is," Alex suddenly pipes up. I didn't even realize she was behind me. "Don't you know who she is?"

"Stop it," I hiss. Sometimes I could kill her.

Mr. Green Eyes, however, looks amused. He raises his eyebrows. "I don't," he says to Alex. "Do tell."

"You're looking at a contestant on *Teen Design Diva*," Alex says. "Just made it past the first round, which is why we're here. She needs inspiration for round two." She is having way too much fun embarrassing me, but I also know she's super proud of me.

Green Eyes looks impressed. "You're going to be on that show? That's awesome!"

I blush. "Well, not yet. I've only made it past the first round of auditions. We'll see what happens in round two. I have to design accessories to complement one of my existing designs."

"Well, then I want to do my part to make sure you make it," he says. "I mean, imagine if you win. I can tell all my buddies at Parsons that I met you before you were famous."

This time, I can tell he's being silly. He winks at me, and I blush again. But, wait, did he just say Parsons? That's only my number-one dream school for fashion design. "How do you know about Parsons? Do you want to be a fashion designer too?" I ask.

"Not exactly," he says. "I'm studying fashion marketing there. My mom is the brains behind these pieces, but I'm her go-to on these travel missions. She likes to stay on the design end, and it's good practice for me." He reaches up to brush a strand of his dark hair from his eyes.

I force myself to stop staring at Green Eyes and focus on the jewelry and stones on the table. After all, that's what I'm here for. The pieces really are exquisite. If you look closely at the stones, you can see crystals reflected underneath. I can feel Green Eyes watching me as I study the pendants.

"How about this?" he suggests, holding up a long brass chain. At the end is something that looks like a little cage, and inside is a reddish-orange sphere with sharp edges. The red reflects out of the cage, casting colored stripes on the table.

"It's cool," I say, "but I don't think it'll quite work. I'm supposed to be creating something, not buying it. And I think I need something a little shorter to keep the proportions in line for the dress I'm accessorizing. I'm leaning toward a statement necklace of some kind." I feel like I should apologize or something, but Green Eyes doesn't look upset, just thoughtful.

"I think I have the perfect pieces," he says. He ducks under the table, and I hear him digging through boxes. When he comes up, he's holding a bunch of clear, crystal stones and metallic studs in a variety of shapes and sizes. The studs all have a cool, vintage look. As he moves his hand, the light hits the stones, making them sparkle.

I'm about to ask him why they aren't on the table with the others, but then I realize why. Each one has little pieces broken off or some other imperfection about it. But for my purposes they're perfect. They have just the right amount of distressing to them. I can already picture a cool statement necklace adding the perfect accent to the neckline of my dress. I can even use them on the shoulders of my dress or along the waistline to create an embellished belt.

"You were right," Alex says to me. "You'll know when you see it." Turning to Green Eyes, she adds, "You have a great eye for detail."

This time he's the one who blushes. "Thanks." He puts all the pieces in a small shopping bag for me, and then takes the cage necklace and puts it around my neck. "On me," he says with a wink.

I gently touch the necklace. "You don't have to do that," I say.

"The stones weren't something my mom could have sold anyway. She won't care. And the necklace . . . well, just wear it on the show," he says. "Mention my mom's designs, if you can." He hands me a card with the words, "Jewels by Liesel" written on it in neat cursive.

I study the card carefully. The name of the line sounds so familiar. "I think I've heard of her," I say.

Green Eyes shrugs. "Yeah? It's possible." He grins, like he's keeping a secret. Maybe he thinks I'm just making that up to be nice.

"Well . . . thanks again," I say, stepping away from the table. I hold out my hand to shake goodbye, and Alex bursts out laughing. I don't know what possessed me to do that. I want to pull my hand back, but before I can, Green Eyes is holding it firmly.

"No problem," he says with a smile. "By the way, what's your name?"

"Um, it's Chloe," I reply. Our hands are still connected, and I know I must be blushing like crazy by now.

"Nice to meet you, Chloe," he says. He stares at me. Am I supposed to say something else? Finally he laughs. "So, you don't want to know my name? I see how it is. Take the jewels and run, huh?"

"No, of course I do. I didn't mean to——" I begin.

"It's Jake," he says. He shakes my hand, and it's only then I realize he is still holding it.

"Nice to meet you, Jake," I mumble, gently pulling my hand away. "And . . . um . . . thanks again."

"Sure. See you on TV," he says with another wink.

I want to say something witty back, but instead I clutch my bag and hurry away.

VARIOUS GOLD CHAINS!

SUPPLIES
AND
Sketches

LONG OR SHORT PENDANT?

NECKLACE
EMBELLISHMENT
Designs

CENTER PIECE
WITH SMALLER
DANGLING
PIECES

STUDDED
& FACETED
WITH CRYSTAL
ACCENTS

Celebrity
CHLOE

VINTAGE GOLD STUDS

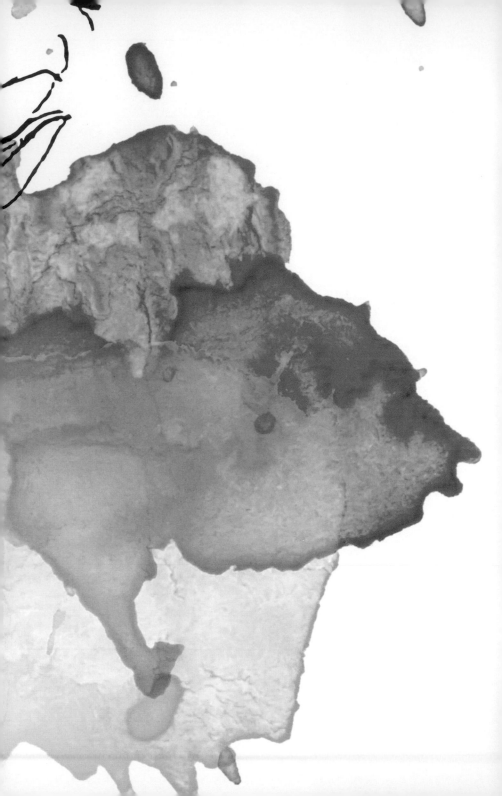

12

It's been two days since the art fair, and I've pushed all (okay, almost all) thoughts of Jake out of my head to focus on my design for the next round of auditions. I've cleared off a section of my floor to use as a workspace and have spread out all the stones and studs Jake gave me. They're even cooler than I initially realized. I have an assortment of pyramid-shaped, spiked, round, and faceted gold studs to work with. In another pile are all my findings for the earrings, bracelets, and necklaces — things like clasps, hooks, and earring posts.

Walking in and seeing the mess would probably throw anyone else for a loop, but to me it's complete organization. I have my own system that just works for me. When I was younger, my mom tried to help me clean up, and I couldn't find anything for days. Luckily she gets me now and lets me keep my room in "organized chaos" mode, as she calls it.

This week the plan is simple — eat, sleep, school, create. Rinse, repeat. It's weird, but I'm less stressed about making jewelry than I am about designing clothes. Maybe it's because it works a different part of my brain or because the patterns are so repetitive. The process calms me.

I carefully take out the thin beading chain I found online and thread some of the larger studs onto it. Then I pick up a small envelope with my most precious stones: Swarovski crystals. After I came up with my design plan, I bought a combination of clear stones in a variety of sizes to add some sparkle. I lace the crystals in between Jake's stones to create a pattern.

I move the mannequin over to my window and hold the necklace up against the neckline of the dress. The sun shines on the crystals and the metallic studs are the perfect accent to my neutral dress. The image, offset by the clean, white background, has the effect I was hoping for. It elevates the dress from everyday chic to an elegant, formal garment. I continue with the beading patterns, but then stop. There's something missing.

I add some larger stones and create a pendant necklace, but as soon as I hold it up to the dress again I know it's not right. With all the gold tones it looks like some kind of Olympic medal — definitely not the look I'm going for. Maybe I need to take a break. Clearing my mind will probably help.

My stomach growls, reminding me that I haven't eaten since lunch, and it's already six o'clock. I smile, thankful to my parents for not interrupting me while I was working, and head to the kitchen.

"Well, well, well, look who's emerged from the Cave of Style," my dad says when I walk in. "I think it's our daughter. At least it looks like her. I'm not sure, though." He makes a big show of squinting and looking me up and down like he hasn't seen me in years. "What do you think?" he asks, turning to my mom.

"Hmm," says Mom. She puts her finger on her chin like she's deep in thought and studies me carefully. Sometimes the two of them are so dorky together. "You're right, it does look like our daughter. But she has this strange look on her face. What would you call that?"

It's like a game of Ping-Pong, and it's now my dad's turn. "Uh, I think they call it happy," he says.

My mom shakes her head and grins. "Oh, then I don't think it's her," she says.

I roll my eyes at them. If I had a pillow, I'd throw it. "You guys are so annoying," I say, laughing.

"Phew," my dad says, "that means we're doing something right."

My mom laughs, and I shake my head at their silliness. "Anywaaaay," I drawl, sitting down at the table to join them. "I'm starving."

The table is filled with my favorite foods: spaghetti, meatballs, and my mom's special sauce. Dad even made garlic bread with three kinds of cheese sprinkled on top of it — his specialty.

I immediately dig in. All that designing has left me ravenous. "This is so good!" I say between mouthfuls. "Thank you, guys."

"You've been working so hard, and we're doing our part in keeping your energy up," Mom replies.

I've really enjoyed making all my designs, but I didn't realize how much I needed to unwind until this moment. I've been going basically nonstop for the past few weeks, which is what I need for the competition, but taking this break is showing me I need to pause more often. If I make it to New York City, the process will be even more intense. I'll have to remember to make Chloe time so I don't crash and burn. Good thing Mom will be there to watch out for me during the competition.

"So when do we get to see your latest and greatest piece?" asks Dad.

"When it's done," I say, smiling.

"Can you give us any hints?" asks Mom.

I tell them about what I've done so far and my arrangement of studs and crystals.

"That sounds really beautiful," Mom says when I'm finished. "I can't wait to see it."

"Thanks," I tell her. "I really like it so far, but it's just not quite there. It still feels like it's missing something. I'm just not sure what."

"You know," says my dad thoughtfully, "maybe you should take a look at some of the old photo albums we have around the house. A lot of your grandpa's old rodeo clown uniforms had really cool, intricate beading. Maybe they'd give you some ideas."

I think back to some outfits I've seen Gramps wear in the pictures. I do remember lots of embellishments on his costumes. Before he died, we went to a ceremony to honor him, and I remember a shirt with beading I liked. I can't remember exactly what it looked like, but I love Dad's idea, especially considering that the third and final round of auditions is going to somehow involve the rodeo. Maybe this will give me a head start if I make it that far.

Dad takes my silence for disagreement. "It was just an idea," he says. "I thought they might offer some inspiration. You don't have to."

"No, no, I was just thinking about it. It's brilliant!" I get out of my chair and give him a kiss on the cheek. "Thank you," I tell him gratefully.

Dad grins at me, and I run to the living room to get out the photo albums. I flip through them, and each time I see something that could work, I make a small sketch of it and write notes about the colors.

When I get to the third album, I finally see exactly what I need. If I can pull it off, my design will guarantee me a spot in the next round for sure.

NECKLACE OPTIONS

13

"So no one gets to peek under the black cloak of mystery?" asks Alex, nodding to the huge black sheet I've put over my new design.

I shake my head. There's only one day to go until the next round of auditions, and I guess I've gotten superstitious. I promised my parents and Alex they'll get to see my design tomorrow, and they've tried to be understanding. For the most part, they've succeeded. But being patient? Not so much.

"I told you, I don't want to risk overthinking it," I tell Alex. "Even if you guys say you love it, and it's the most amazing thing ever created—"

"Which I'm sure it will be," Alex interjects.

I smile at my best friend's confidence in my abilities. "Still," I say. "I can see myself explaining it and then wondering if I should have done something differently."

Alex sighs. "I guess you're right. You do think too much. You need to stop." She throws a pillow at me.

I throw it back. It lands on my nightstand, barely missing a lamp.

"Good thing your dream isn't to play basketball," Alex says. She bends to pick up something that fell on the floor. When she holds it up, I realize it's the business card Jake gave me. I forgot I set it on my nightstand. "Have you looked up this website yet?" she asks.

I shake my head. "I meant to, but I've been so busy making the necklace I just haven't had time."

"You mean to tell me you haven't even thought about how gorgeous Jake is?" asks Alex, rolling her eyes. "Come on, Chloe. I know you better than that."

"Well, I didn't say that," I mutter. "Let's look it up now."

Alex opens my laptop and types in the website address for Designs by Liesel. When the website loads, she frowns.

"What's wrong?" I ask.

"There's nothing here except a photo," she says. "The rest of the page just gives the address of her store in New York City and then says 'Under Construction.'"

I lean over to get a better look. "That woman looks so familiar, doesn't she?"

Alex studies the picture. "Probably her eyes," she says. "They look just like Jake's."

"Yeah, but it's more than that," I say, shaking my head. "I know I've seen her somewhere before."

Alex studies the picture again, too. "You're right. She does look really familiar. Maybe she's a regular at art fairs? We could've seen her at one at some point."

I shake my head no. "I don't think so. Jake said he's the one who usually sells her stuff at the fairs, remember?"

"True," Alex says. "But we've never seen him before either, so you never know."

I keep staring at the computer like if I look long enough the site's 'Under Construction' logo will change into something else. "Oh, well. I give up," I say, closing the laptop. "It's not important, and I don't have time to worry about it now. I have work to do."

"You'll have plenty of time to check out her store when you're in New York City," Alex says. "Maybe that will jog your memory."

For once, I don't correct her use of *when* instead of *if*. Instead, I just work on picturing myself in New York City. It's so close I can almost taste it.

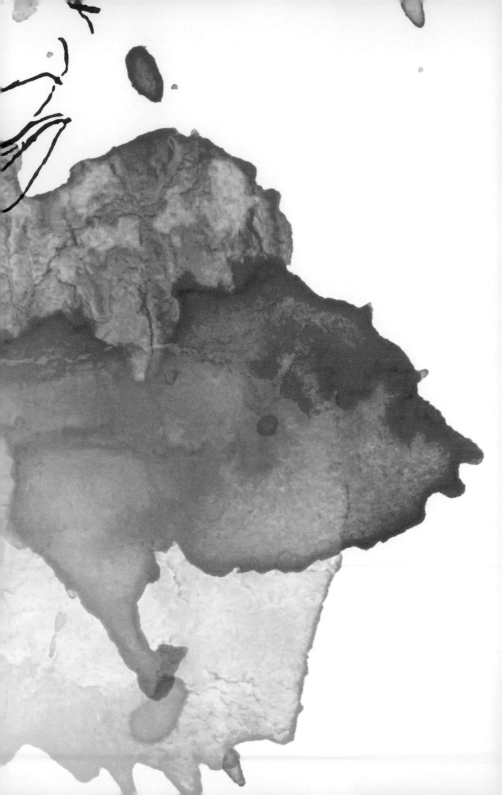

The next day, my mom, Alex, and I drive up to San Francisco for the second round of auditions. Even though there are only seventy contestants left in this round — a major decrease from the hundreds that showed up the first time around — we still get there early.

"I'd rather just get it over with right away than stress about it for another ten hours," I say as we walk in.

"I brought my pillow with me this time," Alex says. She sits down and props the pillow against the wall. In minutes, she's breathing deeply and sound asleep.

"I think Alex could teach us both how to relax more," my mom says.

Alex lets out a low snore as if to prove Mom's point. In minutes, the line has already grown behind us. Apparently I'm not the only one who thought it was a good idea to show up early.

From down the hall, I hear Nina whining to her mother. "This is torture," she complains.

"I'm with her," I say to my mom.

My mom raises her eyebrow. "Never thought I'd hear those words," she whispers.

I shrug. "I think since we both made it this far, we have a truce. I don't know if we'll ever be friends, but I'll settle for not totally despising each other."

My mom pretends to wipe away tears. "My gosh, my little girl is growing up," she says. "I'm so proud of you."

I roll my eyes. "You are beyond corny."

A few minutes later, a producer steps into the hallway. "Chloe Montgomery," she calls. "The judges are ready for you."

I take a deep breath and gather my supplies. I thought I'd be less nervous this time around, but my palms are just as sweaty as they were the first round, and the walk to the stage feels longer than ever. I stand under the hot lights and take the black sheet off my necklace and dress.

When I practiced this in my head, the judges gasped in astonishment when they saw my design. A part of me waits for that, but it doesn't happen. Hunter, Missy, and Jasmine look just as serious as ever.

It's just an act, I tell myself. *They have to look that way.* "Should I start?" I ask.

"By all means," says Jasmine.

I try to remember the notes I wrote down on index cards to help me practice so I don't forget anything. I could have brought them with me, but that would have looked unprofessional. I want every little point I can get.

"The last time you saw this dress," I begin, "it was minimalist but fashionable. For this task, I wanted to bring it up a notch. I also wanted to make some changes to unify the dress with my other designs from the last round and create a more cohesive collection. With the added accessories and embellishments, I can see it worn to a more formal event. And yet it's still not over the top. It has a quiet elegance."

I see Jasmine smile at my choice of words. I reviewed some *Design Diva* clips online and found one where Jasmine said she wished more clothing "possessed a quiet elegance." I took it to mean high quality without the loud bling attached, which is exactly what I was going for with my dress. From Jasmine's smile, it seems like I hit my mark. I hope that's what the smile means, anyway.

"I used the neutral canvas of my dress as a starting point and played with metallics and crystals to add modern touches," I continue. "I also looked back at my other successful design from the first round — the tuxedo leggings and tunic. The leather stripe along the side of the leggings gave me the idea to add leather patches to the shoulders of my dress. The faux leather provides a great contrast to the white of my dress and subtly ties the two pieces together."

Hunter and Missy murmur in agreement, and even Jasmine nods her head. Their reactions add to my confidence. I'm so relieved they seem to like the revised design as much as I do.

"Well said, Chloe," Hunter says. "I can see you've put a lot of thought into this. I love that you looked at the bigger picture and referred back to your other designs. The faux leather accents really tie into the leggings you created for the first round of auditions and add a tough edge to what could have been an overly sweet dress. You're on your way to creating a cohesive collection."

Missy chimes in next. "As you probably know from *Design Diva*," she says, "I'm quite a fan of the bare bones as well. If an outfit has to scream to get my attention, something's not right. The black, white, and metallic color palette you chose just whispers, and it's got me."

"Thank you," I say.

"I can't stop staring at that necklace," says Hunter. "Can you tell us about it?"

"Sure," I reply. "I used a combination of vintage gold studs in different shapes to add dimension and create a pattern. The majority of the necklace is studded and faceted pieces with crystal accents. But it still seemed like something was missing. There needed to be a larger statement piece. I made the center piece a circle with smaller pieces dangling from it, like a dream catcher. I think it really ties all the smaller stones together and gives the necklace a focal point."

"That's really unique," Missy says.

Jasmine laughs. "You always say that, Missy," she says. "No one even knows what that word means anymore because you say that about everything."

Missy looks hurt, and her face crumples like she's going to cry. "You know what, Jazz? Not everyone has to be nasty for no reason," she snaps.

Jasmine waves her hand dismissively. "I wasn't done. I was going to say that I agree with you for once."

"Well, you could have started with that," Missy mumbles.

It's awkward standing up here and watching them fight. I catch Hunter's eye, hoping he'll see that I need some help. He seems to understand, because he clears his throat. "Chloe, I'm really intrigued by the pendant in the center," he says. "What inspired you to make that?"

Maybe it's the stress of the past few weeks or maybe it's just missing my gramps, but my eyes suddenly tear up. I can't help it.

"Oh, good going, Hunter," says Jasmine. "And everyone thinks *I'm* the one who makes people cry."

"No," I say, shaking my head. "It's not his fault." I take a deep breath to collect myself, but when I speak my voice still comes out shaky. "My grandfather was really big in the rodeo world. Back when he was alive, my parents used to take me to see him all the time. When he passed away, we stopped going. I still think about him all the time, though."

I pause and take another breath. "When I was stuck on where to take this necklace, my dad suggested I look at some old photo albums for inspiration. Some of my gramps's rodeo clothing had really cool embellishments. I found this photo of him at the rodeo. He looked so happy, like there was no place else he'd rather be. He was wearing this bolo tie around his neck, and it had something that looked like a dream catcher in the middle. That's what inspired me to create this pendant."

When I finish, I wipe tears off my cheeks. I didn't realize how much I missed my gramps, and I feel stupid crying on stage.

"Dang, girl," says Jasmine, "you made me choke up, too. I don't even have the heart to mess with you. I say definite yes."

"Yes, of course," says Missy.

"Yes, from me too," says Hunter, smiling at me from his seat. "But before I give you your next assignment, which, it seems, is perfect for you, I want to give you some advice. What you just shared with us was gold. Keep that passion and emotion alive and let it guide you throughout this competition."

I nod, at a loss for words. "Thank you," I finally say.

Hunter hands me the envelope with the next assignment, and I walk off the stage. As soon as I leave the auditorium, I race over to my mom and Alex. "I made it to the next round!" I shout, waving the envelope in the air.

"Déjà vu all over again!" yells Alex.

"What's the next assignment?" Mom asks.

"Oh, I haven't even opened it yet." I tear open the envelope and stare at the paper. The words "Rodeo-Inspired Clothing" are printed in big, bold letters.

Hunter wasn't kidding when he said the next challenge would be perfect for me. After my speech about my grandpa, I bet he knew I would love this.

"Awesome!" Alex exclaims, reading over my shoulder.

My mom gives me an excited grin, and I know exactly what she's thinking. Thanks to Gramps, I have this one in the bag.

→ Leather at shoulders!

← Fitted Bodice

Full Gathered Skirt →

Pair with Metallic heels! ↓

Neutrals, Black & White, Gold Accents

NECKLACE FINAL *Sketches*

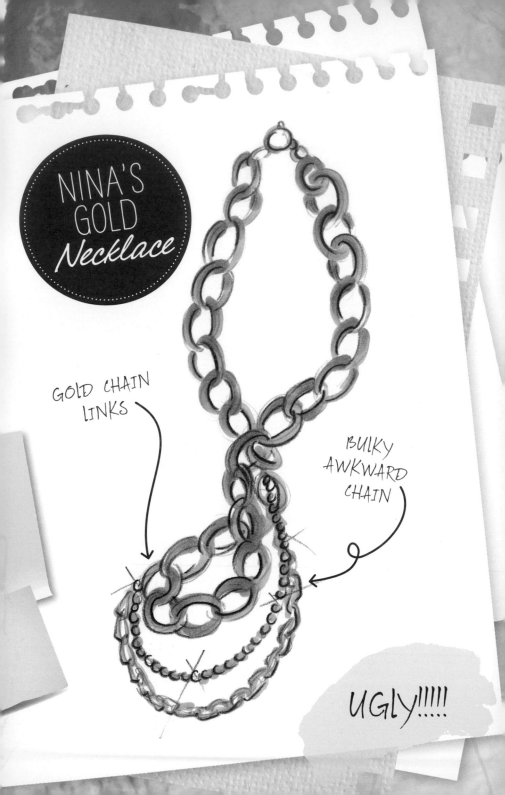

When I arrive at school the next morning, Nina is waiting for me by my locker. She's alone for once — not a single mini-Nina in sight. This time there are no air kisses or fake hugs, probably because there's no audience there to appreciate them.

Nina holds up an envelope identical to the one Hunter handed me at auditions yesterday. "I heard you talking to your mom and Alex," she says. "Looks like we're both in the next round."

"Looks like," I say. "It'll be nice to see a familiar face." I pause. I never thought I'd say it would be nice to see Nina.

Nina must have been thinking the same thing. "Even if it's me, right?" she says. "Don't worry. I feel the same way."

We both laugh. Nina glances down at her feet like she's not sure what to say next. Then, she bends down and takes a small paper bag out of her backpack. "I have something for you," she says, handing me the bag.

Nina is giving me a present? Is the world about to end? "Um, thanks," I say. I stare at the bag, not sure what to do with it.

"Open it," Nina says.

I follow her command, but I'm careful about it. I mean, this is Nina we're talking about. For all I know, this could be a set-up and live snakes might jump out at any minute. I wouldn't put it past her.

But when I peek inside, I don't see any snakes, rodents, or even bugs. I reach into the bag and pull out a long chain made of gold links. It's so long that it reaches down to my belly button.

To be honest . . . it's kind of ugly. The chain looks bulky and awkward, but I can tell Nina is waiting for me to say something. I don't want to lie and say I love it. I think of how Missy described my necklace. "Wow, thanks, Nina. It's definitely . . . unique," I say.

She grins. "I'm so glad you like it. Can you believe it was only five bucks?"

That much? I think. But I force myself to be nice. "What a bargain," I say instead.

"I have it on good authority that the judges like this kind of stuff," Nina says, leaning in like she's telling me a secret. "They call it 'out-of-the-box' thinking."

I want to ask her how she knows what the judges want, but I doubt she'd tell me that part. Nina's parents know all sorts of important people, so it's possible she could be telling the truth.

"Well, I can definitely see how this would fit," I say.

"I got two," Nina replies. "You can even use yours for the next challenge if you want. I might use mine or save it for New York. We'll see. Anyway, this isn't me saying we need to be besties or anything like that." She shrugs and flashes me a smile that looks surprisingly genuine. "I just didn't think it would be fair if I didn't give you a heads-up on what the judges are into. See you later." With a little wave, Nina disappears down the hallway.

"Later," I echo. I put the necklace back in the paper bag and shove it in my backpack. Maybe I will find a use for it, but this challenge won't be the place.

* * *

When I get home that afternoon, I see two trucks parked in front of our house. I take a deep breath and smell food cooking on the grill. My parents didn't say anything about having company, but if it means an impromptu barbecue, bring on the guests.

"There she is, the next *Teen Design Diva*," says my dad as I enter the backyard. "Make way, everyone. Celebrity coming through."

For a change, I go with the attention and curtsy. "Autographs, anyone? I won't even charge you this time. Friends and family discount," I say with a wink.

Everyone laughs. Seated at the table with my mom are two of Gramps's best buddies, Jim and George. We haven't seen either of them in at least a year. I hurry over and hug them both hello. "What are you guys doing here?" I ask.

"We came to help," Jim replies. "Your dad tells us you have a rodeo-inspired challenge coming up, and there's nothing we like more than talking about the good old days, right, George?"

"That's right," says George, running a hand through his gray hair. "Hopefully, our stories can give you some ideas for your designs."

"Rodeo has changed a lot through the years," Jim says. "For the better, I'd say. Back when your granddaddy and I were boys, there were no helmets. Nowadays, they encourage them."

"I don't do much riding these days, but I sure wish they'd required them back in our time. Hit my head so many times, my memory ain't what it used to be," says George.

My dad flips over the meat on the grill, and it sizzles. "Maybe you can do something with that, Chloe," he suggests. "Embellish the helmets to make them look cooler."

Somehow I don't think embellished helmets are exactly what the judges are looking for. Based on the challenge description, it seems like our designs should be more rodeo-inspired than recreations of actual rodeo gear. Plus, I can't imagine macho rodeo guys being psyched to wear a helmet covered in jewels and other embellishments. And even if they were into it, I don't have much experience with headgear. Now is not the time to experiment.

Before I can figure out a way to gracefully decline my dad's idea, Mom speaks up. "What about the clothing itself?" she suggests. "I think that's more Chloe's strength, right, hon?"

I can always count on my mom to be on the same page as me. "That's true," I say, apologetically. I glance over at my dad, hoping I didn't hurt his feelings too much.

He moves the steak to a plate and drizzles it with sauce. "You do whatever you think is best, Chloe," he says with a smile. "I'm not all caught up on my *GQ* quite yet."

I smile. I doubt my dad will ever be fashion-forward, but it's nice of him to try.

"Bring that bad boy right over here," Jim says, getting his fork and knife ready to dive into the steak.

Dad takes another steak off the grill and brings both to the table. Good thing they both were ready at the same time or there might have been a rodeo brawl in our backyard, bull not included.

Jim and George dig into their steaks while Mom and I wait for dad's special blue-cheese burgers. Suddenly, George's eyes light up, and he takes a swig of his lemonade to wash down his food so he can speak. "How about colors?" he suggests. "Our riding gear could certainly use some."

"It's not a fashion show, George. People come to watch the sport," Jim says.

George turns on him. "It *is* a fashion show now, Jimmy, remember?"

Jim's face reddens. "Sorry, Chloe, I forgot," he says apologetically. "I'm a little old school. George is right. Color could sure liven things up."

I laugh at his discomfort. "No worries, Jim. You're right — it is about the sport. But, there are probably fans who come to show off their latest gear, too. So, for them, the costume change would be something different."

An idea begins to brew in my head. I think about the current color palette of tans and neutrals and ways to liven it up. I don't want anything too crazy, but some brighter colors and cool embellishments — fringe, studs, grommets, things like that — could make it more fashionable.

My parents continue to laugh and reminisce with Gramps's friends, but I take my burger and excuse myself to check out Gramps's albums again. I never thought I'd find myself designing rodeo clothing, but after talking to Jim and George I'm feeling inspired. I want to make those outfits so hot that the judges won't know what hit them.

16

I spend the next few days looking at old photos, researching everything I can find about rodeo attire, and trying to get my design plan just right. This challenge is a little unconventional — not entirely surprising since *Design Diva* loves throwing the unexpected at contestants. The judges are always saying they want to see how well they can think outside the box. And rodeo-inspired clothing is definitely outside the box.

George was onto something when he mentioned color. Traditional rodeo gear is usually suede or leather chaps worn over jeans and paired with a button-down shirt. It's a functional combination . . . but not exactly a fashionable one. Still, I know it's important to respect the tradition of rodeo *and* incorporate the judges' theme, so I'm sticking with the somewhat traditional color scheme of brown, blue, gold, and tan. Then I'll spice up the outfit with cool embellishments.

My rodeo-inspired ensemble will feature a much slimmer, more feminine silhouette than the usual uniform. I'm creating a pair of slim, bootcut jeans accented with studded leather fringe. Instead of a traditional button-down shirt, I've decided on a fitted vest with a cinched waist.

It was nice having Gramps's friends here, relaxing and telling stories. It's been a long time since we were so happy talking about him. At least that's how it's been for me. It's hard to talk about him without missing him.

But right now, I try to keep my focus on the happy. I have all my materials spread out in front me — denim for my jeans, several yards of blue plaid for my vest, and all my embellishments.

Today Alex has come over to watch me work. She has her math homework spread out on my floor. She does a problem, then watches me work. Problem, then watch. Back and forth, back and forth, and it's making me anxious.

Finally I sigh loudly. "Stop!" I say.

"I'm sorry, I'm just impatient!" Alex says. "I want to see what kind of progress you're making. Besides, watching you is way more interesting than algebra."

I immediately feel bad for snapping. "Yeah, I know," I say. "I'm sorry. I'm just stressed. This has to be perfect."

Alex makes a big show of oohing and ahhing over what I've done so far. But as she moves around my mess of supplies, she bumps into a can of soda that she's placed precariously close to my pile of fabric. Luckily, she grabs it before it can spill. "Sorry," she says.

"If you had actually spilled it, you'd really be sorry," I say through gritted teeth.

"Tough girl is an interesting look for you," she says, cocking her head like she's examining me. "I can call you Cranky Chloe, or   "

"Alex!" I snap.

Alex sighs. "I need something to do," she says. "I feel so useless."

"You have a math test tomorrow," I tell her. "Study." I know it's mostly due to the stress of the competition, but I'm starting to get annoyed. I definitely don't want Alex to be a casualty of my wrath. "Maybe you should go."

"You need me to save you from yourself, Cranky Chloe," she says as she opens my laptop. She's probably looking up synonyms for cranky that start with C so she can add to my CC nickname. Whatever. As long as she's quiet. I love my best friend, but when I'm working, I need to focus.

I figure out the measurements I'll need for the waist and inseam of my jeans and jot them down. Then I do the same with the measurements for the thighs, knees, and calves. I want to make sure I have everything correct.

Measure twice, cut once — that's what Mimi is always telling me.

Once the jeans are finished I'm planning to add some studded leather fringe along the outside seams. That will provide the perfect modern twist on traditional riding chaps.

To contrast with the dark denim bottoms, I've chosen a bright blue plaid for my vest. As I was studying traditional rodeo gear, the one thing that really stood out to me was how boxy and unflattering the button-down shirts are. I mean, I don't love skintight tops, but I want my vest to have some definition. Figure-flattering and feminine, that's what I'm going for. The updated silhouette done in a more traditional fabric is the perfect combination for this challenge. (I just hope the judges agree!)

I settled on a flattering deep V-neck for the vest, which will be much more elongating on whoever is wearing it, and I'm using cool brass buttons on the front. They remind me of the metal embellishments on the horses' saddles and bridles, which is exactly what I'm going for. I want this to be an elegant take on rodeo-inspired fashion. Not a costume.

I spend the entire afternoon sewing. By the time I take a break, my shoulders ache from hunching over my sewing machine. I hang what I have so far on my dress form and mentally play around with some different Western accessories.

Maybe it needs a belt or something, I think. *Or maybe cowboy boots.* At this point, my brain is exhausted, and I need a break. I don't want to overdo the embellishments.

"Can I help with anything?" Alex asks.

I glance over at her and rack my brain, trying to remember the last time I thanked her for all her help and for putting up with my mood swings lately. Without answering, I get up and go hug her.

"What gives? Is someone dying?" Alex asks.

"I just realized you're the best friend ever, and I don't think I tell you that enough at all," I say.

Alex shrugs. "Aw, girl," she says in a silly voice. "You're going to make me cry." She grins and goes back to her homework, but I swear she wipes at her eyes with the back of her hand.

By the time Saturday rolls around, I'm so nervous I can hardly stand still. I barely slept the night before. I kept having nightmares about embarrassing myself on stage in front of the judges and the entire audience. In one, I was standing on the rodeo stage, and just as I was in the middle of explaining my color scheme, I fell right into the judges, who just happened to be eating pie. Come one and all, and witness the spectacle that is Clumsy Chloe.

My mom, dad, Alex, and I all pile into our car and drive the forty-five minutes to the rodeo grounds in Salinas. The place is already packed with camera crews, booths, food, and rides. This is not typical for June in Salinas. The massive California Rodeo isn't held until the third week in July. There are parades, kids' events, and fairs that take place in the two weeks before that. Basically, July is one big funfest. But this special event to promote *Teen Design Diva* has really drawn a crowd. I guess I shouldn't be surprised — northern Cali does love its cowboys, and everyone seems happy to start the festivities early.

"It's like an appetizer until the real thing comes along," I heard George say the other day.

Just then our car pulls into a parking spot. Everyone climbs out, and I spot George and Jim waiting for us by the entrance.

"Today's your big day," says Alex, giving my arm a squeeze. "Look how many people are here!"

Alex is right. This will be a much larger crowd than the past two rounds. Then it was just the judges. I know she's trying to be encouraging, but suddenly I feel sick. I'm hot. I'm cold. My hands are shaking. My stomach is doing its own version of riding the bronco, and I close my eyes and swallow to stop my breakfast from coming up.

The rodeo is not normally my big day. It belongs to the riders and food vendors and Miss Rodeo California. When I was a kid, I wanted more than anything to be Miss Rodeo. That was until I realized I'm more the design-the-outfits-for-the-pageant type than the beauty-queen type.

Alex must be thinking the same thing because she says, "Hey! You finally get your wish! You can be queen for the day!"

The thought of everyone watching me as I try to explain my designs to hundreds of people almost turns throwing up from an idea into a reality. I quickly lean over and put my head between my knees, taking deep breaths in an effort to settle my stomach. I'm really hoping I don't puke on my favorite boots.

My dad rubs my back, and I pull my hair back from my face, out of the line of fire, just in case. I don't have to look to know that Alex is as far away as possible, trying to focus on anything else. Just the mention of someone throwing up turns her face green.

Thankfully, I manage to not embarrass myself by actually puking, and when I've recovered, we all walk to the entrance. A reporter approaches us, but my dad whispers something to him and he says he'll come back later. I can picture the headline now: "Chloe Montgomery: Sick with Excitement."

When we reach the entrance to the rodeo grounds, Jim, George, and some of my grandpa's other buddies surround us, big smiles on their faces.

"We can't wait to see what Chloe cooked up," George says.

"Speaking of cooking," Jim adds, "some of the best baked beans and sausage I've ever eaten are under that canopy over there. Can I convince anyone to check it out with me?" He points to the Vendor's Row.

My stomach gives another little lurch at the mention of food, but the smells around me are so inviting, I can't resist following Jim. Some of my favorites, like calamari, Philly cheesesteak sandwiches, and Louisiana gumbo call to me, but I decide to start small with kettle corn, cotton candy, and lemonade and save the rest for after my presentation. Nothing like sugar to calm the nerves.

I grab my food and carry it all over to a bench and sit down. The last thing I need is to dump it all over myself before I'm supposed to be on camera. That's *not* how I want viewers to remember me. I concentrate on taking small bites while Alex investigates the rest of the food booths. From my spot, I can see more *Teen Design Diva* contestants arriving and exploring the fair too.

Suddenly a shadow falls over me. "That's quite the breakfast you have there," a guy's voice says. "I didn't realize you were such a health nut."

I know that voice, and so do my palms because they immediately get sweaty. I look up and see Jake grinning down at me. *What's he doing here?* I wonder. But then he sits down beside me, and I lose my train of thought. I

notice he has a big slice of cherry pie on his plate. "You too," I say, nodding at his choice of food.

"Yup," Jake says. "Got my whole grains and fruit, and I bet the crust was made with eggs, too, so I'm counting that as protein."

I look down at my food to see how to spin it. "Fruit!" I say, pointing to my lemonade. "Oh, and corn is a vegetable. We're such health nuts."

Jake laughs. "Hey, I like your necklace," he says.

I put my hand to my throat. I totally forgot I'm wearing the necklace he gave me at the art fair. Figured it might bring me luck. "Thanks," I say, blushing a little. "By the way, the stones I got from you worked perfectly in my design. Got me to this last round."

He smiles and there is that dimple again. "That's awesome. One to go then, right?"

"Yep. Oh, look! They're starting to display the designs." I look toward the stage and see jewelry, boots, and other rodeo-inspired gear being set up. Some of the designs have a lot of embellishments on them — fringe, beading, bright colors, you name it. Others are more muted looking, done in tans and neutrals.

"Which one's yours?" Jake asks.

"The one at the end," I say, pointing to where my plaid vest and fringed jeans are being displayed.

Jake studies the pieces but doesn't say anything.

"Not your style?" I ask.

He shakes his head. "No, that's not it at all. I was just trying to think of a way to describe it, like they teach us in marketing. I like it a lot. My mom will too. It's a really modern take on rodeo."

"Speaking of your mom, I tried looking up her website, but it didn't work," I tell him. "She looked really familiar, though."

"Do you want to meet her?" Jake asks. "She's here, and I bet she'd be really excited to hear about how her designs helped you."

"Sure!" I agree. I quickly wipe the cotton candy from my mouth and hope I look presentable. "Bring it on."

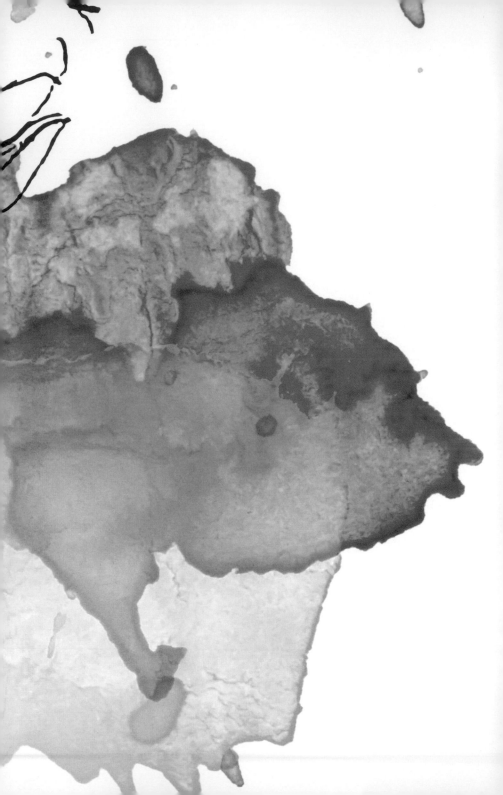

As Jake leads me across the fairgrounds, I see Alex examining some clothes on a vendor's table and motion to her to come along. As soon as she realizes who I'm walking with, her eyes grow wide and she hurries over.

"You have to spill later," Alex whispers in my ear. Thankfully, she leaves it at that and doesn't nudge Jake or ask anything embarrassing.

Suddenly, I see her — Lisa McKay, the season three *Design Diva* winner. She was one of the few winners who really made it big after the show. Not only is her clothing line amazing, but she also has her own jewelry line now.

"Oh, my gosh," I squeal, grabbing Alex's arm and pointing. "It's her!"

Alex may not be much for fashion, but she's as big a fan as I am and immediately sees who I'm talking about.

"OMG!" she says, grabbing my hand. "Lisa McKay!"

Out of the corner of my eye, I see Jake biting his lip like he's trying not to laugh at us. Whatever. I don't care if he thinks we're acting like groupies. It's Lisa McKay!

"I know her," says Jake. "I can introduce you."

My eyes bug out, and Alex and I can't do anything but nod and follow him. In seconds, we're standing next to Lisa McKay's table, and I'm too starstruck to even look at her pieces.

"Hi there, girls," says Lisa, extending her hand. She's so calm and sweet and not unnerved at all by our gawking. She's probably used to silly fangirls.

"Um, hi," I manage to say. I look to Alex for help, but she seems to be at a loss for words for once.

Jake looks at us, waiting for us to say more. When he sees we won't, he takes matters into his own hands. "Mom, this is Chloe, the girl I was telling you about. The one who was really into your designs. And this is her friend Alex."

Somehow Jake's words penetrate my starstruck brain. *Mom?*

Suddenly I realize why I didn't recognize Lisa from her website. In the photo online, her hair is super short and spiky. Now, it's past her shoulders and wavy, just like it was on the show.

Alex finally pipes up and points out the other thing that was confusing me. "But your card says Liesel," she says, clearly just as confused as I am.

Jake's mother chuckles. "That's because Liesel is my name. The producers kept getting it wrong on the show, and after a while I just stopped correcting them," she says with a shrug. "I mean, who cares what they call me as long as I win, right?"

"I owe you big time," I say, finally finding my voice. "Well, you and Jake. Your pieces really put my last design over the top. Thank you so much."

Liesel waves her hand like it's nothing. "I can't wait to see what you did with them. Oh!" She looks at my necklace, clearly just noticing it. "That looks stunning on you! And to think I wanted to chuck it. Shows what I know."

Just then, the static of a microphone interrupts our conversation. We all turn toward the stage and see Jasmine standing there, waiting for quiet. "Designers, we'll be starting in five minutes," she announces. "Please take your seats at the front of the stage."

I let out a nervous, shuddering breath. "That's me," I say. "It was so nice to meet you."

"You too, sweetie," Liesel says with a smile. "Knock 'em dead."

"Good luck," Jake adds. "You'll be great up there. I know it."

Alex and I walk to the stage, and she squeezes my hand. "You're going to be amazing," she says. "Just remember to be confident. Your designs rock."

I take a seat with the other design hopefuls and see Nina is already there. She's the only one I recognize, which isn't that surprising since the contestants have come from all over. We nod at each other. I can tell she's nervous too.

When we're all seated, Jasmine makes her way back to the stage and picks up the microphone again. "Welcome, everyone," she starts. "Let me begin by saying what an honor it is to be here. I know many of you were surprised when you found out about the nature of this challenge. After all, rodeo clothing isn't usually something you'd see featured on Rodeo Drive."

Jasmine pauses, and the audience laughs at her pun. "However, being a successful designer means being versatile, and that's something we want our teens to learn early on. If you want to win this competition, you must be ready to tackle any challenge — no matter how unique. And just like a fashion show, rodeo is a performance. There's an art to it. I hope the forty designs we see today do justice to that."

I like how Jasmine phrases that, combining the beauty of designing and the rodeo. I draw little circles in the dirt with my boots, waiting for the competition to begin. Finally, it's time. The stands fall silent as the first designer takes the stage.

First up is a girl named Daphne Corral. A burst of nervous laughter escapes me as I think about her last name. Corral, rodeo — maybe it's a sign. Her design involves embellishing the existing uniforms with studs, beading, and small gems. It's not the route I would have thought to take, but her result is pretty amazing. She chose earthy tones and used bright blues as accents. At the end, she even makes a joke about her last name, and the crowd laughs.

The next contestant, whose name I don't catch, freezes on the stage. I can totally sympathize. When she finally speaks, she describes the mauve she chose as periwinkle and gets flustered. Missy tries to talk soothingly to her, but it doesn't seem to help much. In the end, Hunter has to explain most of her pieces, but it's clear he doesn't fully understand what she was going for.

One by one, more designers take the stage, and the crowd filters in and out. It takes a long time to go

through forty designs, but the contestants and their families don't move. We all want to see the competition. Some of the designs I like, others I don't, but it's hard to tell which direction the judges will lean. Everyone's taste is so different. That was obvious the night Jim and George came over.

Soon, it's Nina's turn. Even though she seemed nervous before, you can't tell from her confident strut to the stage. Nina chose to change the color of the rodeo clothing and decided to use various shades of green in her design. The judges ask her about her color choices, and she says she focused on greens "to be one with nature." That's so not Nina, but I doubt anyone will know or care. All that matters is how the designs look, and even though it pains me to admit it, hers is one of my favorites.

Finally, there's only one designer to go before it's my turn — a guy named Derek Bonnell. Derek walks easily to the stage, but he doesn't strut like Nina did. He chose to focus on the boots for his design, which is not an easy task. I love to buy shoes, but I definitely don't attempt to make them. Derek talks about how he dyed the leather and stitched the looped design on the side. He also did something to the sole of the boot to add traction.

Derek's functional alteration gets some approving buzz from the rodeo riders in the audience. Up until

now, the designs have focused on the aesthetics, not anything functional.

It's amazing to be a part of this and witness so much talent, but to be honest, I'm getting a little discouraged. I like my designs, but there are *so* many good ones here. What sets each one apart? What is that one thing that will make the judges choose mine?

"Thank you so much, Derek," Jasmine says. "We have one design left to go. Let's welcome Chloe Montgomery to the stage."

I smile and don't realize I'm not moving until my mom leans forward and gently nudges me. I don't remember walking to the stage, yet suddenly, I find myself looking out into hundreds of faces. The sun beats down on my skin, and I clear my throat. *Speak, Chloe, speak*, I think.

Suddenly I see Jake give me a small wave from the audience. I see my parents and Alex smiling and giving me encouraging thumbs-up signals. I take a deep breath. Confident Chloe is back. I can do this.

19

"It's nice to see you again, Chloe," Missy says. "Tell us about your design."

I've answered this question about all my other designs so far, and I'm ready with an answer. "I think the rodeo attire used today serves a purpose, but from what I heard from some riders, the uniform could use some spicing up," I begin. Who cares if *some* was really *one*? There have to be others who agree. Whoops come from the audience, so apparently there are.

"My grandpa was very involved in rodeo, so honoring the tradition of the sport was really important to me," I continue. "When I was planning my design, I wanted to create something that acknowledged that but added a modern twist. That's why I decided to use a traditional color palette but create something with a slimmer silhouette. I also added studs and fringe to embellish the outfit."

Jasmine nods. "Why did you decide to add the studs and the fringe?" she asks. "Did you not think the jeans were enough on their own?"

This question throws me off, and I try to read Jasmine's expression. Is she purposely trying to stump me or does she hate my idea? I must focus on her a little too long because I see the audience shifting and getting restless.

I sigh. Who knows what she's really thinking? I'll just answer honestly. "Actually, I toyed around with a few ideas. I didn't want to use too many embellishments because I wanted my design to be wearable — not a costume. The fringe and the studs provide the perfect balance. They're interesting without being too over-the-top."

Hunter leans forward in his seat. "What I like about this is the comfort you've shown with embellishments. I mean, from what you told us previously, that's not usually your thing, right?"

I hear my family and Alex laugh in the audience. "True," I say, smiling, "but the rodeo is different. It's massive. It deserves a little flash and sparkle."

"Thank you so much, Chloe," Missy says as the crowd applauds and whistles. "We'll take a short break as we discuss all these wonderful designs, and then we'll announce who will be continuing on to the competition in New York."

I walk back to my seat, feeling good. I did my best. Now all I can do is wait.

* * *

An hour later, I'm starting to realize that waiting is easier said than done. I explore the booths to pass the time and even manage to down some gumbo, which is just as fantastic and spicy as it was in the past. But as good as the food is, it can't distract me for long, and I end up making my way back to my front-row seat to wait.

Once I'm seated, I look around at the other contestants. Everyone tried so hard, but only fifteen of us will make it to New York City. It's not easy having that next step be so close, only to have it fall through. I clench my hands into tight fists as if that can stop the win from slipping through my fingers.

Just then, Jake slides into the seat next to me. "You were great up there," he says. "My mom thought so too."

It's great to hear that Jake liked what I had to say, but knowing Liesel McKay liked my designs is really cool. Assuming he didn't just say that to make me feel good, that is. "Thanks," I reply.

"Someone said Garrett Montgomery was your grandpa," he says, sounding impressed. "I didn't know that."

"Well, I didn't realize you followed the rodeo," I reply with a shrug.

"My dad is big on the scene," Jake says. He points to a man in the crowd, but I don't recognize him. Then again, I really only know my grandpa's friends, and Jake's dad is on the young side. "I've been hearing about your grandpa since I was in diapers. He seemed like a good guy."

"He was," I say. "Thinking about him helped motivate me to get here." I look to the stage, but there are still no judges. "It's been more than an hour. I wonder how close they are to making decisions."

Jake nods to the side of the stage, and I spot Missy walking toward the microphone. "I think they're about to tell us," he says.

Everyone else must have been scoping out the stage too, because the crowd quiets down before Missy even has a chance to speak.

"Usually, we drag things out far longer," Missy starts, "but there are some delicious-looking sandwiches and pie calling my name."

The crowd laughs. "Don't forget the sausage and gumbo!" someone shouts.

"Oh, I won't, sugar," Missy says. "This belly is starved." There's more laughter, and she waits for quiet before she continues. "First I want to say that this was not an easy decision. We have forty very talented designers here, and it would be wonderful to see every rodeo rider in one of their designs, but unfortunately, we can't do that. The lucky fifteen we choose, however, will see their designs displayed at the California Rodeo next month. So without any further ado, Hunter and Jasmine will read the names of the teens who will be going to New York City to continue their quest for the fashion internship."

Jasmine and Hunter walk onstage, each carrying a list of names with them, and begin to read them off. The crowd cheers for each one, and the winners run to the stage. Derek and Daphne are both called, and halfway through the list, I hear Nina's name. The list continues, and I'm counting the numbers — they're up to fourteen designers now. I can't even figure out the order. It's definitely not alphabetical, or I'd have been after Nina.

"One more name, ladies and gentlemen. My apologies to Missy and her stomach, but we're going to drag this out a little more here," Hunter says.

Missy clutches her stomach and looks longingly at the food vendors.

"The last contestant going to New York City gave me some pause in the beginning," Jasmine tells the crowd.

"That could be anyone," I mumble.

"She's had some highs and lows," Jasmine continues.

Hunter grabs the mic away. "One low, Jazz, not some," he corrects her.

Jasmine rolls her eyes. "I'm trying to add suspense. Anyway, she's had more highs than lows. How's that?"

"Much better," Hunter says. "This designer really touched us with her family story."

At that, I perk up. That could be me! Hunter told me they liked me talking from the heart. I feel my mom's hand squeeze my shoulder from behind.

"Oh, for heaven's sake," says Missy, taking the microphone. "I can't stand it. She's from Santa Cruz."

When she says this, the crowd goes wild. I glance behind me and see my family and Alex jumping up and down. What if there's someone else from Santa Cruz? I desperately try to remember if there's anyone else besides Nina and me.

"Chloe Montgomery!" the judges shout. "Come on up here!"

OMG. I can't believe it! Did they really just say my name? I feel like I'm in a daze, and then someone's hand is on my back, pushing me forward. I run to the stage and find myself engulfed in a hug with all the other contestants and judges. I feel like I'm dreaming and have to resist the urge to pinch myself. Am I really going to New York?!

Cameras are suddenly in our faces, and the reporters surrounding the stage are shouting questions at us. How do we feel? Did we have a feeling we'd be the final fifteen? What do we think about New York City? Everyone is talking at once, and the reporters try to get all our names down.

"Nina and Chloe," a reporter yells, "we've been following your story from the beginning. Now you're both headed to New York City. Is there really no rivalry there?"

I open my mouth to say it will be nice to see a familiar face in New York, but Nina cuts me off. "I guess time will tell, right?" she says.

The reporter raises his eyebrows. "Interesting," he says. "And you, Chloe, what do you want to say about your journey?"

There's so much to say, I don't even know where to start. "It's been incredible," I say. "I've learned I'm capable of much more than I thought and to not let things stand in the way of my dream." That sounds a little cheesy and rehearsed, but it's true.

"Well said," the reporter replies, eating up my words of wisdom. "Now let's get a photo of our Santa Cruz girls."

Nina looks wary, but when a photographer steps forward, she puts her arm around me and pastes a smile on her face. When the flash goes off, I'm grinning from ear to ear. Who cares if I'm hugging Nina? I made it. New York City, here I come!

I can't believe it. I'm finally here. New York City.

Everything has been a total whirlwind since the last round of auditions. I packed my bags, and my mom and I headed to New York City for the remainder of the competition.

There's so much energy and craziness everywhere. The city is all taxis honking, people yelling, and lights flashing. It's different and scary, but thrilling too.

I look around our hotel lobby, the meeting place for the *Teen Design Diva* orientation. The letter delivered to my hotel room said all fifteen contestants should meet here. Everything looks so elegant — the marble floors, the plants hugging each corner of the room, and the soft, beige leather chairs. The other contestants are gathered nearby, and I recognize a few people from the earlier rounds of auditions, but the only person I really know is Nina. Given our history I'm not exactly anxious to go talk to her. I wonder if everyone else is feeling just as nervous and excited as I am.

Just then, the elevator doors whoosh open, and Missy, Jasmine, and Hunter walk into the lobby. They're followed by a camera crew. Even though I've met them in person multiple times now, my heart still starts to race at the sight of them.

Missy smiles warmly at all the contestants. "First of all, we'd like to welcome all of our talented designers to the Big Apple. Even if you're from New York City or have been here before, I guarantee this competition will be like no other experience you've ever had. When things get tough, remember to keep your eye on the prize — an internship with one of the city's top designers. It's an opportunity every designer dreams of, and it could be yours." With that, Missy waves Jasmine forward.

Jasmine's stilettos click on the floor, all business, as she steps to the front. "Let's get the important stuff out of the way. As I'm sure you already know, you'll be in New York for one month. There will be a total of seven challenges, and two contestants will be eliminated after each challenge. The show will be taped, except for the final elimination, which will air live. All the challenges will be timed, and unless stated otherwise, you will be allowed to use only the materials we supply." Jasmine turns to Hunter. "Anything else you want to add?"

"Be creative," Hunter says, smiling at the group. "Use your strengths, but don't be afraid to try something new. Think outside the box."

At this last suggestion, I feel a poke in my back. I can't be sure, but it's probably Nina saying I told you so. That's exactly what she said the judges were looking for when she gave me that weird necklace back home. Looks like she was just being nice after all.

"And remember," Missy adds, "have fun!"

"Your first challenge will be held tomorrow morning at nine o'clock in the Central Park Zoo," Jasmine tells us. "Your packets have maps as well as walking and subway directions. Don't be late."

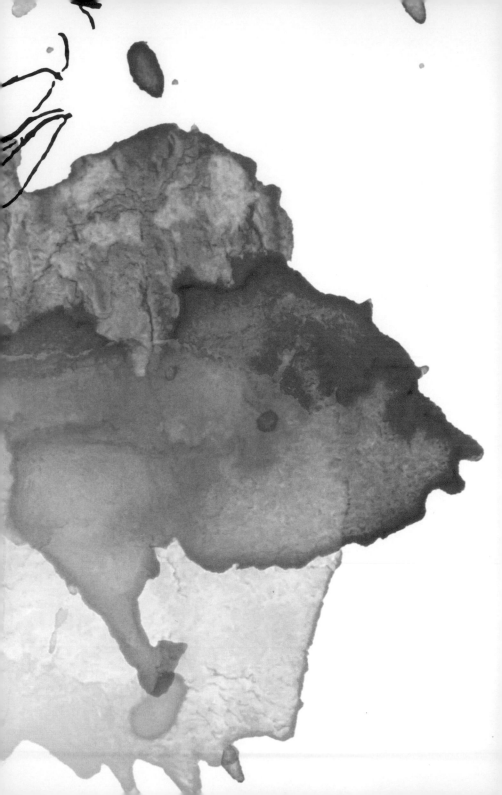

The next morning, I'm up and out of bed bright and early — partially because I couldn't sleep, but also because it was clear Jasmine wasn't kidding when she told us not to be late. Seems like everyone else felt the same. All the other designers, along with their parents, gather outside the entrance to the Central Park Zoo at nine o'clock on the dot. The judges, producers, and camera crew are already there waiting for us.

"Fifteen for fifteen," says Jasmine, looking pleased. "We're off to a good start."

"For your first challenge, you'll have one hour to explore the zoo," Hunter says. "Decide what you'd like to see most. We'll meet back at the garden when you're done and explain more then. Choose wisely."

Everyone splits up to explore. Mom and I pass the zoo's Tropic Zone. Exotic birds chatter excitedly in the trees, and I make a mental note of the brightly colored feathers. As we move to the back of the zoo, monkeys screech at us from above as they swing from vine to vine.

I wonder how the zoo is supposed to play into our designs. Will we have to make clothes for animals? That would be a little out there, even for this show.

My mom and I come to a stop in front of the snow leopard cage. Inside, the big cats are snoozing lazily. "They don't seem to be fully awake yet," Mom says.

I point to the description posted beside the cage. "It says they're nocturnal. It must be too early for them too. Maybe we can come back."

We move on to the Polar Circle, and soon I'm watching polar bears, penguins, and other sea birds. The penguins waddle to get a fish dangling from a zookeeper's hand, and the polar bears bat a huge ball around in the water. It's so easy to get lost in the animals' games. One polar bear does a loop around an ice tunnel and comes out the other end.

I notice some of the other designers gathering around and watching too. We all have notebooks and phones to jot down ideas, but none of us do. It's hard to know what to take notes on when we don't know what we'll be designing. From the corner of my eye, I see my mother glance at her watch and frown.

"How much time do I have left?" I ask.

"About fifteen minutes," she replies.

"We should probably start walking back," I say. I'm a little nervous that I haven't seen enough yet, but I'm more nervous about being late.

My mom and I cut through the center of the zoo, past the sea-lion exhibit. Trees separate the area. Small clusters of rose bushes bookend the trees — pink roses with yellow in the center, lavender ones with white accents, and red ones with white and yellow inside. In the center of the area is a large pool. Sea lions are sitting on the rocks around the water. Others are jumping into the pool.

"Sea lions are very social animals," a trainer is explaining to a group of contestants standing nearby. The sea lions bark and clap their flippers in agreement, and the trainer throws them a treat. Another sea lion does a flip in the air before diving back into the water.

A redheaded contestant claps his arms, sea-lion style, and the other contestants and chaperones laugh. "Where's my treat?" he calls. An identical redheaded boy standing beside him, obviously his twin, elbows him in his ribs.

As I watch, the sea lions race around the pool. Their sleek, dark bodies look elegant as they glide through the water like underwater ballerinas. A moment later I glance up and see the judges have gathered beside the rose bushes. Time's up. I can only hope what I saw brings me the inspiration I need.

I head over to where the judges are waiting, and the rest of the contestants follow suit. While we were exploring, the producers assembled several racks of clothing and a table covered with a sheet.

"Ladies and gentlemen," Hunter says, "you had some time to explore, and we hope you were paying attention. Because your first challenge will require you to use the animal exhibits as inspiration."

Oh, man. Maybe they're going to make us design clothing for the animals after all, I think.

"Your challenge is to think about your favorite exhibit and create a garment that reflects that," Jasmine says. "But there's a twist. Because there are no electrical outlets available to us at the zoo, that means no sewing machines. This first task will simply be hand sewn."

I try not to groan. Of course there's a twist. I should've known they wouldn't go easy on us just because it's the first challenge. Hand sewing will make things that much harder.

"You will be given three hours to complete your design," Hunter continues. He points to the rack, and I notice the basic shirts, skirts, pants, and shorts hanging there — stuff I'd lounge around the house in. "As you can see, there's nothing glamorous about these pieces. Your task is to change them from drab to fab. Add a fancy hem. Dress something up with ruffles. The sky is the limit as long as you make it work."

I try to take a deep breath and think clearly. Back when I first started sewing, I used to do this kind of thing all the time. Transform my clearance skirt with a cool embellishment or a funky hem. I should be able to come up with something in three hours, right?

"And last but not least," says Missy, "you'll be able to use all this!" She pulls the cover off the table to reveal dozens of fabrics and embellishments.

Around me, I hear the rest of the designers gasp. Whatever apprehension we have about this task is momentarily replaced with awe at the assortment of materials.

"Impressive, right?" Missy says. "Take it all in, but watch the time."

I ready myself, one leg in front of the other, as if I'm about to start a race. Jasmine raises her hand and looks at her watch. "Your time. Starts. Now!"

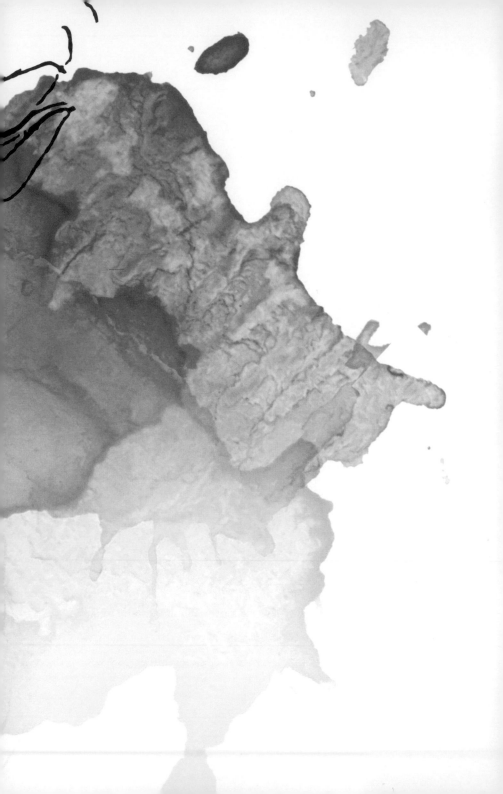

22

A handful of contestants immediately run to the shelves, but I hesitate. How can I get started when I don't know which exhibit I want to focus on? The monkeys were kind of interesting. Not sure what I can do with them, though. The leopards were promising, especially with their stunning fur, but all they did was sleep. Penguins? Polar bears? The sea lions?

I look around me, trying to come up with an idea. I don't want to do anything too crazy since we have limited time and no sewing machines. Those constraints make things pretty difficult. Suddenly it hits me. The garden! I can make something inspired by the nearby flowers. It might not be animal-centric, but it *is* a zoo exhibit.

My idea starts to take shape as I browse the shelves and racks. A white T-shirt immediately catches my eye. It's super plain right now but perfect for this challenge. I grab it off the rack and start sketching. While I think of how to dress it up, a breeze picks up and the smell of roses hits my nose. I use colored pencils to sketch a ruffled rainbow collar — that will definitely make the shirt anything but ordinary. I hold the paper in front of me. It's definitely unique. In fact, it'd be perfect — if I was designing for a clown. I bite my lip and check the clock. I have still have more than two hours left, but I want to make sure I leave myself plenty of sewing time.

Just then, a cameraman moves closer to me and zooms in to take a close-up of my disastrous drawing. I was so focused I'd almost forgotten about the cameras surrounding us. I try to shield my paper a bit. That quick sketch is *not* how I want to introduce myself to viewers.

Around me, half the designers have already started sewing. The other half of the group is still sketching, but I have no way of knowing if their first attempts are as lackluster as mine.

I stare at the plain white T-shirt in front of me. I definitely want to use ruffles to simulate the delicate petals of the flowers in the garden, but how to incorporate them? I don't want to do anything too cheesy or amateur.

What if I ditched the sleeves? A halter top would look a bit more refined. And keeping it all one color would help.

I quickly eliminate the sleeves from my sketch and tweak the neckline. Then I add soft, white ruffles along the neckline in a bib design. They'll mimic the flower petals from the garden and also frame the face of whoever is wearing it.

I take a moment to study my sketch so far. Success! Now all I have to do is execute my design. With no time to waste, I attack the shelves for supplies: needles, scissors, thread, and some white chiffon for the ruffles.

I pick a spot beside a tree and lay out all my materials. Cutting off the sleeves is the first step so that the creation doesn't look like some weird T-shirt hybrid. Then I can use the chiffon for the flower petals. I quickly cut off the sleeves to create the new silhouette, then get to work hemming the frayed edges.

When I've finished that task, it's time to add the ruffles. They're what will really tie the shirt into the zoo's garden. I try not to think about my sewing machine back home. Things would be so much easier if I could use the ruffler foot on my machine. The special attachment creates ruffles in seconds and is one of my favorite machine-sewing tricks.

"Designers, you have one hour left," Hunter announces to the group.

Only an hour left!? Where did the time go? I think frantically.

I quickly trace the shape I'll be cutting out onto the chiffon. The lightweight material is perfect for this application — the movement of the material mimics the flower petals perfectly. I hold the chiffon up against the front of the T-shirt and think through my plan of attack. The ruffles need to have some volume, otherwise they'll just flop around. I start pinning the fabric in place, bunching the ruffles up so they don't lie flat, and start sewing. There's no time for fancy stitching. I just have to make things stay put. I attach them along the neckline and down the front. The rough edges of the chiffon give the shirt a cool, modern look. My fingers work quickly, and my wrist gets tired. I use a running stitch to make fixing mistakes easier, and it's enough to hold the ruffled petals in place. If I had more time, I would have used something sturdier, like a cross-stitch, but then I'd be stuck if I messed up.

"Thirty minutes!" Hunter says from behind me. I jump a little. *How long has he been standing there?* I wonder.

Hunter moves over to someone else, but now I'm feeling a little frazzled. The thread rips in my fingers, and I try not to panic. I can do this. I thread the needle again and try to concentrate, blocking out everyone around me and focusing on the thread and ruffle. In and out, in and out — ouch! Stupid needle.

A cameraman moves in closer to capture what I'm working on. I try to stay focused, but it's almost impossible to ignore him. My needle moves quickly as I finish attaching the rest of the petals. When I'm done I hold up the T-shirt and want to cry.

The petals look like they've been attached to the shirt completely haphazardly. The finished product barely resembles my original sketch. The petals are limp, and anyone with halfway decent eyesight will be able to see the crooked stitching. The threading is straight in some spots and completely jagged in others.

"And time!" Jasmine calls. "Designers, put down your needles and thread."

I sigh. There's nothing I can do now except hope for the best. But I'm getting a little worried that my best might not be good enough.

ZOO
DEVELOPMENT
Sketches

ANIMAL-INSPIRED
DESIGNS

FUR
SHAWL

silk
satin
gown
beaded

SILK VEST
W/FUR
HOOD

Tulle skirt
w/scattered
beads

SEQUIN
TOP

SILK
cargos

FUR
TRIM
BOOTS

FLOWERS, RUFFLES, GIRLY

HORIZONTAL
RUFFLE T

TIGHT
"PETAL"
T

BOW
RUFFLE
HALTER

LOOSE
PETAL
T

KEYHOLE
T

RUFFLE
HALTER

FABRIC
FLOWER
+LEAF
with stem
stitching

RUFFLE
"BIB"
T

Judgment time. I grab my lackluster top and join the rest of the contestants in a line in front of the judges. I have a feeling this is going to be painful.

Jasmine, Missy, and Hunter start at one end of the line. I peek around to see who will be first. It's a girl with dark hair and shockingly pink bangs. I think she was the one who used studs and jewels to liven up the rodeo uniforms in the last round of auditions.

"Daphne, tell us about what you chose to make," Jasmine says.

"Um, I was inspired by the tropical rain forest," Daphne says, sounding a bit uncertain. I guess I'm not the only one feeling nervous about this first challenge. She holds up a rainbow-colored pencil skirt that has feathers dangling from the hem. "Specifically all the tropical birds. I chose to liven up what was a plain Lycra skirt with bands of color and feathers."

"I appreciate your bold use of color, Daphne," Hunter says, "but I'm not sure the feathers are working for me. They're a bit much with the bright colors. I think this is a case of less being more."

The judges move down the line asking everyone the same questions: *What inspired you? Why did you choose these colors?*

When they get to Derek, it's obvious he's blown them away — just like he did in the final challenge in Salinas. His drab clothing of choice was an oversized purple V-neck shirt. He's managed to turn it into a chic dress with a fitted purple top and a leather skirt on the bottom.

"My dress was inspired by two different areas — the children's zoo area and the sea lions," Derek tells the judges. "The different textures represent all the hands-on things in the children's zoo, and the faux leather fabric I choose for the bottom half of my dress reminds me of the sea lions."

When I crane my neck to study Derek's design, I see how seamlessly the skirt is attached to the shirt. It's a chic, color-blocked masterpiece.

"Very creative, Derek. Thank you," says Hunter, running his fingers along the stitches before moving on.

The judges are getting closer. They've made their way over to a girl standing a few feet away from me. I have a good view of her design, and it looks like it might be a kilt. Was it supposed to be a kilt? It's hard to tell because there is no obvious stitching on the plaid fabric she chose.

"Stefanie," says Missy, "what can you tell us about your design?"

Stefanie sniffles. "I had to unravel the whole thing," she says, looking at the ground.

Jasmine frowns at her. "So you just have the fabric?" she says.

"Yes," says Stefanie, "but I can tell you what it was supposed to be."

"That won't be necessary." Jasmine sidesteps Stefanie and moves on. "Luke," she says as she presses on her eyelids with her fingertips, "please tell me you were able to do something."

"I did something," Luke whispers, his shaggy hair falling into his eyes. "This was going to be a dress." He holds up a gray linen cloak with cross-stitching in the center, and I try to imagine the dress that could have been.

Jasmine takes another deep breath. I can tell it must be killing her not to lash out at Luke, but it's only day one. "But it chose to become a cloak instead?" she asks tightly.

"Yep," says Luke.

"Well," says Missy, "at least you have something that can be used, right?" She pokes Jasmine in the ribs, but Jasmine shakes her head and walks over to me, totally tuning out Luke's explanation about which zoo exhibit he was inspired by.

As Jasmine comes to a stop in front of me, my heart starts pounding and my palms start sweating. The cameras focus on me, and I try not to look as panicked as I feel. At least I have something, right?

"What do you have for us today, Chloe?" Jasmine asks. Her voice is desperate, like she's begging me not to disappoint her.

"I was thinking about the gardens all around us when I made this ruffled shirt," I say. "The chiffon ruffles I added to the neckline were inspired by the flower petals, and I opted to stick with white fabric to keep things clean and monochromatic."

Hunter nods approvingly. "I like that you reimagined the T-shirt's silhouette; you're one of the few designers to do so. I also appreciate that you've stuck with your style aesthetic in terms of the neutral color. And the stitching is very precise here."

I smile and nod as he, Jasmine, and Missy huddle together to inspect the shirt. *Don't panic*, I think. *Maybe they won't notice where you messed up.*

"Not so precise here." Jasmine points at the wild sewing.

Busted. I open my mouth to explain, but what can I say? I ran out of time? I messed up? I'm sure they can figure that out themselves. The judges walk away, and Jasmine doesn't look happy.

The judges continue their critiques, and soon there are only five designers left — Nina and the two sets of twins in the competition.

Next to me, Luke scowls. "I thought we each had to make our own designs," he says.

What is he talking about? I wonder, looking around. *The twins didn't work together, did they? Wouldn't that be against the rules?*

Jasmine sends a stern look in Luke's direction. "Of course everyone is responsible for his or her own designs," she says. She turns back to the twin brothers. "Sam and Shane are aware of that, right?"

They nod, and Jasmine turns to the twin sisters beside them. "Jillian, Rachel? Separate designs each task." The girls nod too. "Splendid," Jasmine says. "Then let's keep going."

Sam explains that the polar bears' arctic exhibit inspired him to stitch embroidery on a simple white shirt. I leave my mannequin to check out his stitching. There is not even a smidge of faulty sewing. Each pattern is carefully crafted, and it's hard not to be jealous. Yes it's simple, but it's immaculate.

Not to be outdone, Shane took a pair of boring khaki pants and changed them into business shorts. "I was inspired by the trainers' outfits," he explains. He expertly stitched the hems to prevent fraying and added intricate embroidery to the belt area. If I didn't know better, I'd say the twins had a sewing machine stashed nearby.

"Fabulous," says Missy, unable to contain her excitement. "I love the idea of dress shorts. It's very chic."

Sam and Shane fist bump and grin at each other. Next to them, Rachel and Jillian giggle nervously as the judges move over to inspect their pieces.

"I was inspired by the Arctic Circle too," says Jillian, pointing to a bright-blue, high-waisted skirt. "This originally had buttons and a zipper, which I removed to make it more elegant. I also added fabric to create a wrap belt and embellished it with crystal studs, which remind me of snow."

Before the judges can finish admiring Jillian's skirt, Rachel launches into her explanation. Jillian narrows her eyes at her sister, annoyed that she's stealing her spotlight. "My design," Rachel says, "was inspired by the lions." She added brown leather panels to a denim dress, giving it a jungle feel.

That's thinking out of the box, I realize. She didn't let the fact that the lions were sleeping stop her. She thought beyond that. Why didn't I?

"Very creative work, ladies," says Hunter. "And last, but certainly not least, Nina."

Nina looks confident, but I'm not sure if it's real or an act. "As you can see," she says, "I sewed a white shirt to a high-waisted black skirt to create a two-toned dress. It's an homage to the penguins."

Homage? I think, stifling a laugh. Definitely an act. Who talks like that? Just then I see a camera focused on me. Oops. I hope they didn't catch me laughing at Nina.

Nina explains that she changed the crew neck collar into a V-neck to help elongate the garment. The idea is similar to Derek's, but the designs are leagues apart. Where Derek's stitching flowed seamlessly, Nina's is visible and jagged.

The judges run their hands across the fabric, studying it quietly. Finally, Hunter says, "I can see where you were going with this, Nina, but the execution could use some work. Your stitching is very uneven in several different places."

Nina nods, no longer smiling. I know how she feels, but I think we'll be safe for this round. The fact that our designs were finished should keep us safe from elimination.

"Thank you, everyone," says Missy. "The judges need to deliberate for a bit. When we come back, we'll let you know who's safe and which two designers will be sent home."

With that, Hunter, Jasmine, and Missy disappear into a nearby building. The rest of us look at each other, but no one says anything. I glance down at my design again. I really need to budget my time better for the next challenge. If watching *Design Diva* has taught me anything it's that there are going to be lots of insane challenges. I'll have to learn to do what Rachel did and see beyond what's there.

Just then, the judges emerge from the nearby building. All the contestants look eager and nervous. Missy seems a bit dejected as she takes her place in front of us. "We understand this was the first challenge, and

OTHER CONTESTANTS' *Designs*

JILLIAN'S SKIRT
WITH BOW

DAPHNE'S SKIRT
WITH FEATHERS

DEREK'S DRESS
WITH LEATHER SKIRT

we wish we could have given you more time to get used to the process," she says, "but rules are rules."

Hunter nods. "We also know that what we see now will improve dramatically by the end of the competition," he says.

"However," Jasmine adds, "we have to work with what we have." She turns a page in her notepad. "In the top five, we chose designs that truly impressed us. Designs that didn't make us think, 'this could have been truly great with more time.'"

I swallow. My design is definitely not in this category.

"If I call your name, please step forward," Jasmine says. "Derek, Sam, Shane, Rachel, and Jillian — congratulations! You're in the top five. That means that in the next challenge, you'll have first choice of materials. You'll also be given extra planning and sewing time."

Sam and Shane fist bump, the girls hug, and Derek gives his dad a thumbs-up. I try not to groan. All five of them made amazing designs this round, and time wasn't even an issue. I can't imagine what they'll be able to create next time around with extra sewing and planning time on their side.

"Unfortunately, we also have a bottom five," Jasmine says to the group.

I remind myself to breathe as she starts listing off names. In the bottom five are Stefanie and Julia, neither of whom finished their designs; Luke; and two guys named Tom and Curt. Thankfully, I'm safe.

"Again, we know the time constraints were hard," Missy says. "But we still have to let two of you go. Stefanie, Julia, because you weren't able to make any sort of design, you'll be leaving us today. I'm sorry."

As the eliminated designers step forward, I catch Nina's eye. She shrugs and makes a disappointed face. Stuck in the middle of the pack was not how either of us wanted to start off the competition. But right now, survival is what matters most.

Two days after the zoo challenge, I stare at the note that was slipped under our hotel room door early that morning. I read it for about the hundredth time:

YOU'VE ALL WORKED SO HARD AND DESERVE SOMETHING SWEET, SO JOIN US IN THE LOBBY AT ONE O' CLOCK FOR A DELICIOUS TREAT.

"This can't just be a treat," I say. "It has to be the next challenge."

My mom sighs. "I know, Chloe, you've been going on about it all morning. But you won't know until you get there. Go check it out."

I throw down the note and head downstairs. There are no judges to be seen, just hungry contestants and a towering display of mini cupcakes. They're all beautifully decorated in pastel frosting with gold and silver flecks along the edges. Edible pearls adorn each swirl.

I choose a dainty pink one. It takes two bites to finish. Next, I pick a green one with silver flecks. The taste is a surprise: key lime with custard in the middle. Yum! After two days of worrying about how I can get into the top five, this is a welcome break.

Speaking of the top five, I realize that Derek and the two sets of twins are nowhere in sight. Are they off strategizing somewhere? I see Luke and the two other boys from the bottom five sitting together too. The reality shows I watch are all about forming alliances.

Is that what people are doing? I wonder. *Should I be joining up with someone too?* But before I have time to worry about it, the judges arrive.

"Ladies and gentlemen," Hunter says, "I'm glad to see you're enjoying your treats, but on this show, things aren't always what they seem. And today, a cupcake is not just a cupcake — it's also your inspiration. For this next challenge, you will have to create cupcake-inspired headpieces."

I knew it! Cupcakes with no strings attached were too good to be true.

"Headpieces?" Luke calls out. "I thought this was a clothing design competition."

Jasmine smiles tightly. "In the design world, it's important to be versatile. The best designers have range. We want to see yours. So if it can go on your head, it meets the requirements."

"Be creative," Hunter continues. "You have three hours to complete this task."

I still don't see the twins or Derek. Even if they are currently my biggest competition, it doesn't seem fair to have them miss this task.

Jasmine seems to read my mind. "Some of you may have noticed that the top five designers from the last challenge are missing. That's because as part of their prize, they got a head start. They're already hard at work behind these doors."

I'd totally forgotten about the extra time the top five won. Hopefully, there's still plenty of good fabric left. My goal is to budget some planning time, then sew, sew, sew. But first, I need a design. What's cute and feminine like a cupcake? A bow! I can make a cool hat with a killer bow. In green. Like key lime pie. It's not necessarily my style, but it definitely fulfills the headpiece requirement.

Wait, is that too easy? I wonder. I rub my temples. I can't overthink it. I've seen plenty of *Design Diva* competitions where contestants were so busy second-guessing themselves and their designs that they ended up with disastrous outfits. Or worse — nothing at all.

Jasmine and Hunter walk over and open the double doors. The top five designers are already hard at work inside and don't even raise their heads when we walk in. They are too busy stitching — by hand.

No sewing machines again? I think. This task keeps getting better and better.

In front of us, I see shelves covered with bolts of fabric. There are also sewing supplies arranged in baskets beside the shelves. It looks like there's one basket for each designer, so that will make the organization easier. At least I won't have to waste time racing around for supplies.

"I hope those cupcakes gave you some ideas," Hunter says. "Because time starts now."

I find a spot in the corner and whip out my sketchpad. I quickly draw the design for my bow, then run for the shelves. I'm almost there when someone elbows me in the ribs — hard. I double over and try to catch my breath. When I look up, a camera is zoomed in on me. "I'm fine," I say to the camera, getting back up.

"Accident! Sorry!" Nina calls as she rushes back to her station with her supplies in hand. Whatever. There's no time to wonder about whether she's telling the truth. I race to the shelves, and my eyes zero in on the shimmery green satin. I grab that, along with some lighter green fabric, a hat form, and a needle and thread..

Since I know what my fabric looks like now, I add details to my sketch. I sit with the materials, trying to get a feel for the fabrics. My machine would have let me complete this task quicker, but this design is doable.

I grab a glue gun and add glue dots to the satin before pressing the lighter material to it. Once I scrape away the extra glue residue, I fold the edges of the satin over and in, holding them in place with my finger.

I roll my neck and squeeze my shoulder blades together. Sitting hunched up is killer. When I look up, camera lights blink at me from each corner of the ceiling. I know this will be televised, but seeing the reminder of that fact while I'm working makes me a little nervous.

Ignore it, Chloe. Head in the game, I tell myself.

Time to scrunch and sew. I squeeze the center of the fabric into an exaggerated bow shape. Now to stitch the middle together so it will stay in place until I make a loop. I pull the thread tight with each stitch so the middle is sewed firmly together.

"Ninety minutes!" Hunter calls out.

I can't believe half the time is gone. The bulk of my headpiece is done, but I still need to add the finishing touches and attach it to the hat form. While the glue gun is reheating, I sneak a look at what everyone else is making. Last week's top five designers are huddled in one area, sewing like crazy. Even with extra time, they don't seem close to finishing.

In another area, Nina looks like she's making some kind of clip, but when she sees me looking, she covers her design. Like I would copy her. The judges made it clear that identical designs would result in elimination. Then there's Luke, who looks like he's doing more eating than designing. There's a suspicious smear of frosting on his lip. I don't know whether to feel bad for him or laugh. Maybe he's just a fast worker and has extra time to eat.

Getting back to work, I measure the width of the hat form I chose and pick a piece of green fabric to cover it, making sure it's large enough to fully cover it. Then I wrap it around the form, attaching it to the underside with glue. Holding the ends firmly in place, I count to thirty in my head and then release my fingers. Once the fabric feels dry, I carefully attach the bow I created.

I glance up at the clock. Done, with five minutes to spare.

INSPIRATION:
KEY LIME CUPCAKE

CUPCAKE FINAL *Design*

Bow/Ribbon Accent

CUPCAKE DEVELOPMENT *Sketches*

FLOWER FASCINATOR

"Nice bow," says Nina as we walk to the center of the room to display our designs.

I can't tell if she's being serious or sarcastic. "Thanks," I say, deciding to give her the benefit of the doubt. I look at her design, a pink barrette decorated with small, red stones. It's simpler than my design. "You too."

Nina doesn't say anything. Maybe she's just too preoccupied with the judges, who are already fawning over Derek's hat. His hat is an elegant replica of a cupcake done in black netting.

"Derek," Missy says, "I don't know how you put this together in such a small time frame, but I am impressed. There's minimal stitching. The rest is fabric spray? Glue gun?"

"Both," says Derek.

"Can't tell," says Hunter. "Good job."

It is impressive. Now I'm really envious of the extra time the top five designers had. Luke is up next, and the contrast between the two designs is glaringly obvious.

"What," begins Jasmine, "is this?"

"A headband," says Luke. "It combines three different fabrics, which represent the different colored cupcakes, and can be worn inside out too."

Luke's idea is definitely simple. I can think of several things he could have added to it   for example, he could have stitched more fabric to one of the sides to make them more distinct or embroidered a section. What he created probably took an hour max. Which would explain how he had time for his cupcake feast.

The judges walk to the next competitors, and I look at Luke. He's smiling. I guess he figures as long as he's not eliminated, it's all good. I think of my dad's favorite expression: you can't have your cake and eat it too. Luke sure proved him wrong.

"That's just not acceptable!" Jasmine is suddenly yelling.

I crane my neck to see what she's so mad about. My mouth drops open when I see Beth's and Zoe's "designs." Both sewed a few pieces of fabric together and then smeared cupcakes all over it.

"Explain," Jasmine sputters. "Now."

Beth grins. "It's an edible veil. In the art world, it's called avant-garde."

Jasmine stares her down, but Beth doesn't blink. "And what's your story, Zoe?" Jasmine demands.

Zoe giggles. "Edible hat."

"It's like you two tried to outdo each other for worst creation," Jasmine says through clenched teeth.

When the girls say nothing, Jasmine looks to the double doors, like she's ready to storm out. Instead, she stalks over to Sam and Shane, the twin brothers who were in the top five in the last task.

"Can you tell us about your design?" Jasmine asks Sam.

"I call it the anti-cupcake fascinator," Sam explains. "I focused on using shades of orange and black to add mystery. Then I attached fabric to the back to create a retro tie-back visor."

The way he combined his colors still makes me think of cupcakes, like side-by-side Halloween ones. Yet, he took the design to another level. He didn't see the pastel colors and think they were his limit. Maybe that's what will set his design apart.

"I really like that you didn't just take the task at face value," says Hunter.

Turns out Shane, Rachel, and Jillian didn't either. They did have more time than everyone else, but

RACHEL'S CUPCAKE *Design*

CUPCAKE INSPIRED: HAND-SEWN FLOWERS WITH PEARL CENTERS

DETAILED & PRECISE

Floral Appliquéd Fascinator

thinking beyond the task is what distinguishes their designs. Shane created a reversible knit hat and shaped the fabric to resemble a cupcake. Jillian constructed a headscarf with a 3-D cupcake design. It's not something I would wear. But I can't deny the high level of difficulty.

"My headpiece," Rachel says, "was inspired by the yellow-and-white cupcake. The colors reminded me of a daisy so I used the beading and fabric to create appliquéd daisies with pearl centers."

Missy inspects the hand-sewn flowers Rachel made and is clearly impressed. They're so precise, I have no idea how she finished in the time limit. I am *not* looking forward to being judged after her. My design would have been more impressive after Beth and Zoe's edible art.

"Hi, Chloe," says Hunter as he approaches. His blue eyes are mesmerizing under the bright lights of the camera crew. "Tell us about your design."

"It was inspired by the key lime cupcake," I say. "The volume of the bow on the hat was inspired by the frosting on the cupcakes, and I used different textured fabrics to enhance its femininity." Did I really just say all that? It sounded like a catalogue description.

Hunter nods. "Good choices. I appreciate that you took inspiration from the cupcakes rather than just replicating them. Nicely done."

I let out a sigh of relief as the judges move on to Nina's barrette, which Missy calls "unique" and then Tom's heavily beaded hooded scarf, which Jasmine rules "overdone." The last designer is Curt, who was in the bottom of the pack with Tom and Luke in the zoo task. He used wool to make a cap, which looks a little plain to me.

When everyone has presented their designs, the judges excuse themselves to go discuss. Tom, Luke, and Curt finish off the last of the cupcakes while the top-five group plays cards. Beth and Zoe hold up their edible creations and vamp for the cameras. I think about approaching Daphne, but she looks like she wants to be alone. Same goes for Nina, who's busy studying her nail polish.

Oh, well, I think. Waiting for judges makes me nervous, and I'd probably say something dumb. I count the ceiling tiles instead. Before I can get too far, the judges return.

"Okay everyone, you know the drill from the last challenge," Hunter says. "Let me start by saying we were very impressed with some of your pieces."

"And much less impressed with others," Jasmine says, pointedly looking at Beth and Zoe.

"Derek," says Missy, "your design was amazing. Shane and Sam, we continue to be wowed by your creative flare. Rachel, the flowers on your design were detailed and precise. And, Jillian, while we differed on exactly where your design could be worn—"

"And by whom," Jasmine mumbles.

"We were all in agreement on the level of skill," Missy finishes. "You are the top five and safe for this round. Congratulations! For the next challenge, you will not only have additional work time, but you'll also have the opportunity to choose a new challenge if you don't like the one you're assigned."

Sam and Shane fist bump again, but this time they bring Derek, Rachel, and Jillian into the fold.

"Unfortunately, that brings us to the bottom five," Missy says. "Two of you will have to leave us today. Daphne, while we adored your belt, the task was to make a headpiece. So, unfortunately, you are in the bottom five. And, Luke, we're afraid the cupcakes served as inspiration for your stomach rather than your design. You're also in the bottom five."

Luke smiles sheepishly and licks his lips.

"Tom," says Hunter, "we liked your idea of the hooded cloak, but the beading was way over the top."

"Which brings us to Beth and Zoe," Jasmine says. "Ladies, I'm not sure what you were thinking, but it's clear you did not take this challenge seriously. You are both in the bottom five for this task."

I let out a sigh of relief. I wish my design was top-five worthy, but at least I'm safe for another challenge.

"I could stretch this out, but I don't think it's much of a mystery," says Hunter, looking at the bottom five. "Smashing cupcakes on material is neither avant-garde nor abstract. It's lazy. Beth, Zoe, you're both dismissed."

The girls actually giggle, which annoys me. *Why go through all the trouble of getting here if you don't care about the competition?* I wonder. Before they walk off, they blow kisses to the camera. I guess that explains it. They're just there for the cameras.

Everyone heads to the elevators, looking relieved to have survived the challenge. I spy Jasmine and Missy chatting with a couple of the top designers. I'm relieved too, but I'm also disappointed. Being a stuck in the middle isn't good enough. I want to crack the top five.

At the elevator, Hunter taps me on the shoulder. "Chloe?" he says.

"Yes?" I say, surprised.

"You're almost there," Hunter says. "Push a little harder and I think next time around a top-five spot will be yours." Before I can reply, he's gone, offering no more advice for what it is that will move me to the next level.

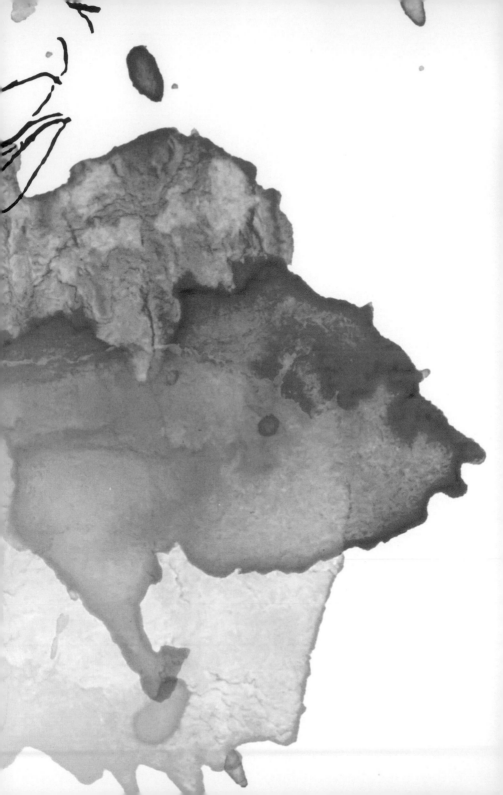

The next morning, I beg my mom to let me explore the city on my own. After making me promise to text her every thirty minutes, she gives in. Thank goodness! I need to think, but I also have a mission — I want to find Liesel's store. As a previous *Design Diva* winner, I have a feeling her store will be beyond impressive. I take out the business card Jake gave me and notice the necklace he gave me is also in my purse. I put it around my neck. Maybe that's the problem — I was missing my good luck charm.

It looks like the subway will be fastest, but it's an unfamiliar maze, so I decide to walk the forty blocks to Liesel's store. That's a rookie mistake, because by the time I get there my legs are aching. After texting my mom to let her know I'm alive, I flip through the racks. There are handbags, scarves, and wraps, all adorned with Liesel's signature jewelry pieces.

If I had to choose a favorite *Design Diva* success, it would definitely be Liesel. Not only was she consistently in the top five during her season, but when the show ended, her designs became so popular that she was able to branch out and create a line of jewelry and accessories.

I flip through the racks, passing over the same pieces again and again. Just then a voice says, "Find anything inspiring?" and I look up into Jake's green eyes.

"Just poking around," I say, trying to ignore the butterflies in my stomach. If I'm being honest, I was hoping I'd run into him here.

Jake takes his backpack off his shoulder and sets it on the floor. "How's the competition going?"

"It's going," I say with a frown. We're not allowed to reveal the outcomes of any of the challenges. All the contestants had to sign a confidentiality agreement as soon as we got to New York.

"That great, huh?" Jake says.

I shrug. I'm not even allowed to tell him if I'm still in the competition or not.

"Oh, right, you probably can't tell me anything, can you?" Jake says. "I remember that from when my mom was on the show."

"I'm sworn to secrecy," I tell him. "Sorry, it's a little frustrating. I can't talk about anything."

Jake snaps his fingers. "You need a change of scenery, some inspiration. Want to go for a walk?"

Suddenly my legs don't ache as much as before. "Sounds good," I say. "Let me just text my mom. It's been a full eight minutes since I last checked in." I roll my eyes.

Jake laughs. "My mom was the exact same way when I first visited her in New York. It gets better."

"Visited?" I'm confused. "I thought you lived here."

"I do now," Jake replies. "But when my parents first divorced, I stayed with my dad to finish school. My mom moved here." He swings his backpack over his shoulder, and we walk in the direction of my hotel. "Now that I go to school here, it's my mom's turn to have me all to herself."

We walk quietly for a few minutes because I'm not sure how to segue from divorce to competition strategies. Finally, Jake breaks the silence. "Smile! You're in New York! You should be excited!"

I laugh. "I am excited. It's just a little overwhelming at times." I hesitate for a second. "Can I ask you something?"

"Ask away," Jake replies.

"What was the hardest thing for your mom?" I ask. "During *Design Diva*, I mean."

Jake thinks for a minute. "Probably the challenges. Some of them were pretty out there." He laughs. "For one, she had to make a collar inspired by deep-dish pizza."

"I remember that!" I say with a laugh. "Someone used real sauce."

"Yup. Jasmine was less than thrilled," Jake says.

"The problem with crazy challenges," I begin, trying to be careful what I say, "is that it's impossible to connect to them. Like how does pizza scream fashion?"

"Well, assuming you're still in the competition," Jake says, raising an eyebrow, "think about the last round of auditions. The rodeo-inspired clothing. You had a lot of passion when you described those designs."

I throw my hands up. "Yes, because I cared about those things. How am I supposed to be passionate about peng—" I stop and clamp my hand over my mouth.

Jake grins. "Whatever task they ask you to do, you have to find a way to be passionate about it. Think of something about yourself you can bring to the challenge."

"That's easy for you to say," I mutter.

Jake looks surprised. "It sounds like you're already giving up," he says.

I stop walking. Jake's right. I do sound like I'm giving up. But I'm not. I don't think I am, anyway.

"Look," says Jake, "I'm not saying it's not hard. My mom had a really tough time with the pizza task. She was in the bottom five. But the next challenge she came back stronger than ever. You have to make that connection."

"You're right," I say quietly. My phone buzzes, and I groan. Mom, of course. "I'd better get back. My mom is freaking out." I text her that I'm on my way back to the hotel.

When I look back up from my phone, Jake is holding two mustard-covered soft pretzels. He hands me one, and I take a big bite. Yum! "Thanks for listening," I say.

"Anytime," Jake says. "You can do this — assuming you're still in the competition, that is."

I smile. "And if not, then the next time around, right?"

Jake suddenly pulls out his phone and snaps a quick picture of me. "What's your cell?"

I rattle off my number, and Jake sends me the photo. I laugh when I see the mustard on my lip. "Are you planning to sell this to the tabloids when I'm famous?" I ask.

Jake pretends to look shocked. "How did you know?"

My phone buzzes again. This time it's Hunter, telling us to meet in front of the Toys "R" Us in Times Square in one hour for our next challenge.

I sigh. Back to reality. "I have to go," I say. "Tell your mom I said hi."

"Sure thing," Jake says. "I'll text you."

"Only words of wisdom, please," I say.

"Here are the first ones," says Jake. He types something into his phone, and a moment later mine buzzes. I look down to read his text — "Make a connection."

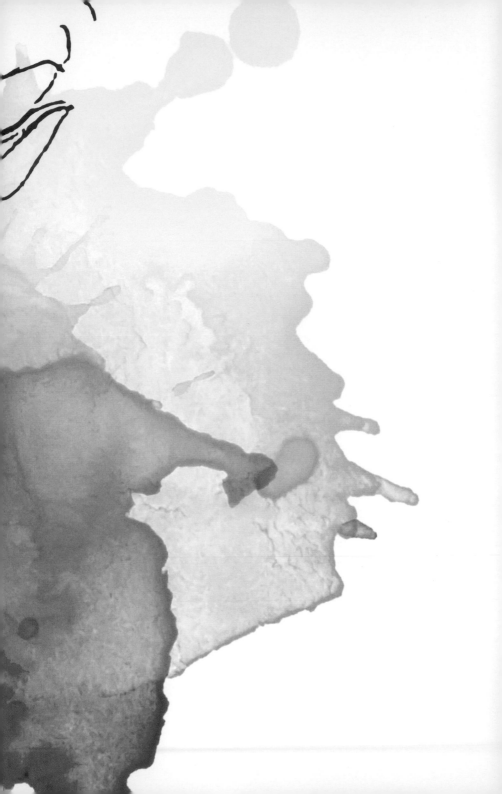

Times Square is like its own little world. Crowds of people swarm the blue road, which is blocked off from traffic. I push my way through and head over to Toys "R" Us, where the judges, camera crews, and some of the other designers are already waiting.

"Welcome," Jasmine says when we've all gathered around. "I have some good news for you today. Starting with this challenge, you will have access to sewing machines."

That is good news. Maybe access to a sewing machine will be what makes the difference for me in this challenge.

Jasmine looks at her watch. "It's almost one o'clock. You'll have an hour and a half to explore Toys "R" Us before you start designing."

"Needless to say," says Missy, "your next challenge will be derived from what you see. The store speakers will announce when it's time to regroup for the challenge instructions."

With that, Hunter opens the doors, and all the designers run into the store. It's enormous — at least three levels high. I follow the sound of roaring, and in minutes, I'm standing in front of a massive dinosaur replica straight out of *Jurassic Park*. It stalks and roars amid a backdrop of mountains and forests, striking fear in passing children.

I take a picture with my phone and move on to a Lego exhibit, almost bumping into the Incredible Hulk. He's bigger than I am and made entirely of Legos. I snap another photo and text it to Alex. Lego building was always her specialty growing up. She made sure the tiniest details, like eye shape and window designs, weren't forgotten. I can't forget those little touches in my designs too.

Candy Land is my next stop. There are giant candy canes and sugarplums just like in the board game and bin after bin of candy. While I'm debating what color jellybeans to buy, my eyes wander to the center of the store. As soon as I see the massive Ferris wheel, I know where I'll be spending the rest of my time.

The Ferris wheel sits smack in the middle of the store. The line to get on is long, but I snag a spot. I need to experience this ride. Every car on the wheel is unique. There's one that looks like a taxi, another built to resemble a school bus, and some that have movie characters. No two are alike. When it's my turn, I choose the one with Mr. Potato Head. It sails into the air, and I can see all the parts of the store. I snap more photos and think about the Ferris wheel that's erected at the fair back home every summer. It's one of my favorite times of year.

By the time the Ferris wheel touches back down, I'm inspired. I sit in a corner, flip through my photos, and jot down ideas and inspiration in my sketchpad. When I hear the announcement that all the designers are due back at the front of the store, I'm calm. Whatever spin the judges put on this challenge, I'm ready.

I look at the text from Jake again. Connection made.

28

"I'll keep it short and sweet since I'm sure you're all eager to get started," Hunter says. "The theme of this challenge is 'The World Is a Toy Store.' Interpret that however you want, but be sure to use one or more store sections as a starting point." He takes out a box with slips of paper inside. "The item you will have to design is on these slips of paper. Take one, but don't open it."

We each take a paper. "Derek, Sam, Shane, Jillian, and Rachel — you were all in the top five last week, so you may open your papers first," Hunter continues. "As part of your prize, you have the opportunity to switch garments. But keep in mind that there is no guarantee you'll like the alternative better. So how about it? Does anyone want to switch?"

Four contestants shake their head no. Only Derek raises his hand. "I'd like to switch," he says. "With Chloe."

Me?! I think frantically. *But he doesn't even know what I have! How is he so sure it's better? Or maybe he thinks I can't create whatever he has.* But there's nothing I can do. I frown and hand over my paper.

Derek looks at it and smiles with satisfaction. I try to push down my annoyance. Now is not the time to lose it.

"You'll have three hours for this task," Hunter says. "Last week's top designers will get a thirty-minute head start to choose fabrics and start designing. When they're done, the rest of you may start. The clock starts now."

The top five immediately start sketching furiously. I look down at my new slip of paper and try to get back in my happy zone. No matter what it says, I can do it. There's no wall separating us from the top five today, and I watch them sort through the materials, flinging pieces every which way. When I see something with potential, I make a mental note to remember where it is. Finally, just as Derek sits down at a sewing machine, Hunter calls, "And go!" to the remaining six designers.

We race to the sewing machines. I place my sketchpad and phone beside me before opening the slip of paper.

SKIRT. I almost laugh with relief. That's perfect! The Ferris wheel reminded me so much of the fair back home, and with Candy Land added in, I have the perfect inspiration for my skirt — cotton candy!

Even though the top five got to choose fabrics first, the shelves are still fully stocked. I immediately spot a bolt of tulle in a soft pastel pink. Perfect! That's exactly what I need for my cotton-candy skirt. I'll need a lot of yardage to create the volume I'm looking for, so I grab the entire bolt, plus a pink knit for the lining. Then I grab some elastic. I'll use that to create a cinched waistband to contrast the volume of the skirt. Finally, I grab some sparkly gemstones to add embellishment and tie in the whimsy of the toy-store theme.

It's time to get to work on the tulle. I measure and cut eight knee-length pieces of tulle so my skirt will have plenty of volume — that's key for my cotton-candy inspiration. Then I cut the pink knit lining so that it's the same length as the tulle and as wide as the hips on my dress form plus about ten inches.

Keeping an eye on the time, I get to work on the hem of my skirt. I sew the short sides of each tulle layer together using a French seam to keep the edges looking nice. Then I do the same with the lining.

One hour down, two hours to go. Around me, sewing machines are whirring. I'm almost at that point too, but I want to get it just right. It would be possible to make a no-sew tulle skirt, but I want to take advantage of the machines. A hack job is not going to cut it today.

Cotton-Candy
Design

FITTED
WRAP TOP

CASCADING
GEMS

FERRIS WHEEL!

TOYS "R" US
DEVELOPMENT
Sketches

Next I get to work matching up the seams and top edges so I can baste the layers of tulle together. It's a painstaking process with so much tulle, since it's hard to see each individual layer when they're all on top of each other, but it's important to get it right.

Be patient, I remind myself. *Take your time.*

Once all the tulle is basted into one piece, I pleat and pin the top edge so that it's the same width as the knit lining. I alternate sides to try and keep my pleats even. Then I match up the top edges of the tulle and lining, making sure both fabrics are right side out, and baste the two together to hold them in place temporarily.

I quickly measure the waist of my mannequin and cut a piece of elastic to fit. My skirt is meant to be high-waisted, so I measure for a snug fit around the smallest part of the mannequin. Putting the two cut ends together, I race over to a sewing machine and stitch them together to create an unbroken circle of elastic.

Time to put the two pieces together. I grab my skirt and some pins and mark half-, quarter-, and eighth-inch measurements around the top of the skirt and the elastic, then pin the waistband to the fabric at the marks. Finally it's time to sew. I hold the elastic and tulle together and put the pieces through the machine. They go in easily, which is such a relief from the painstaking stitching I had to do on the previous tasks. In minutes, the fabric is sewed, and I examine the neat threading. I'll never take a sewing machine for granted again!

Light from the cameras suddenly shines in my face, and I try to block it out. I need to put the finishing touches on my skirt.

"Forty-five minutes!" Jasmine calls.

It's crunch time. I grab the gems I selected and start attaching them to the tulle. My fingers work quickly as I sew them on, being careful not to rip or tear the fragile material. I place a greater concentration of gems and studs at the top of the skirt, near the waistband, and gradually lessen the embellishments as I move down the skirt, creating a cascading effect.

With fifteen minutes left, I slip the finished skirt over the top of the dress form and step back. It looks exactly as I imagined. The fullness of the skirt reminds me of the soft cotton candy I buy every year at the fair back home, and the added gemstones cascading down from the cinched waistband give it a fun, whimsical feel. I can already picture it with a snug, cropped sweater to balance the proportions of the skirt. Maybe in white or black to add drama and sophistication.

For the first time since I arrived in New York, I feel confident. This is my winning piece.

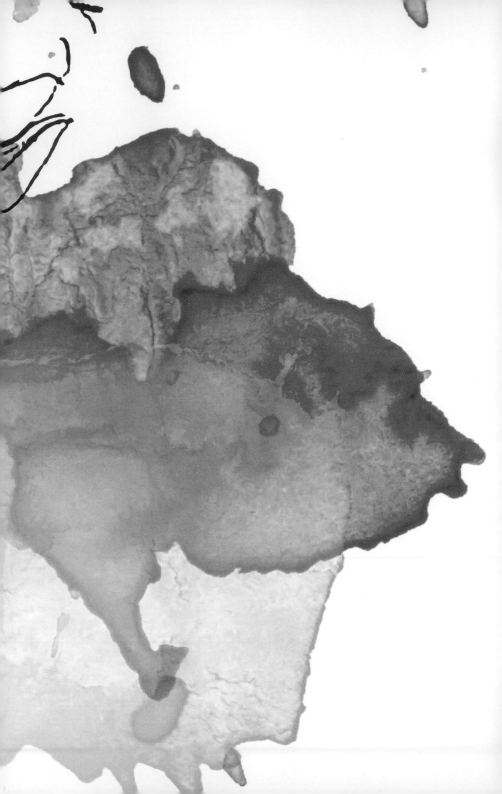

29

Jasmine moves from one design to the next, looking them up and down silently. She pauses at each one, jots something down on a piece of paper, and keeps going. Missy and Hunter follow her, taking their own notes. When they reach the end of the line, they look up — their signal to let us know they're ready.

"Let's start with the end of the line for a change," says Jasmine, moving to stand in front of Derek.

I haven't had a chance to peek at his design, but I've been dying to know what it was.

"You switched assignments with Chloe. How do you feel about your decision?" asks Jasmine.

"Great," Derek says. "I wasn't in a skirt mood today. Chloe's assignment was a blouse, and I was up for the challenge. I was inspired by the *Jurassic Park* section of the store and found this army green rayon with a subtle fatigue print that really represented that. The sheer, delicate fabric provides a good contrast to the pattern, and I added faux leather detailing on the shoulders to really amp up the contrast. The texture of the material reminds me of the giant dinosaur replica."

Jasmine feels the material and nods. "This is beautifully made, Derek," she compliments him. "The fabric drapes so well, and I love the contrast between the sheer airy material and the faux leather."

Derek tips an imaginary hat in thanks, and the judges love it. I'm sure they'd be happy to stand and talk to him all day, but they move on. Tom is next, standing in front of a blue jean jacket. "My garment was a jacket, which I chose to make out of denim," he explains. "It's my nod to the Super Mario Brothers."

Jasmine checks out the denim jacket. "The stitching is a little obvious and I'm not in love with the oversized buttons, but it's fine."

Nina is next, and she's bouncing in anticipation. "I used the Ferris wheel for inspiration," she blurts as soon as the judges pause in front of her.

I have to fight the urge to roll my eyes. Great minds think alike, I guess. I just hope she doesn't have the same

238

explanation as I do. Especially since we're from the same hometown.

"My garment was a skirt," Nina continues.

Oh, come on! I think. *We both have skirts and chose the Ferris wheel as inspiration? What are the chances?* I crane my neck to see her design and sigh with relief. At least there are no similarities between our designs. Nina created a floor-length, A-line skirt in black with a red heart pattern along the hem. It reminds me of construction paper hearts from grade school. It looks so forced. Usually, her designs are more chic.

"And how did the Ferris wheel play into your design?" Missy asks.

Nina blushes. "I had my first kiss on the Ferris wheel, and I wanted people to think of love and romance when they looked at this skirt."

What? I think. *That is so not Nina — and so not true!* Nina is terrified of Ferris wheels. I know for a fact that she's never even been on one. She's been scared of heights ever since we were little kids. I narrow my eyes, and she smirks. Anything to win, huh? I think back to Nina elbowing me during the last challenge. That seems much less of an accident now.

"Awww!" Missy exclaims, and I have to fight the urge to gag.

Once the judges have gotten their fill of Nina's artificial sweetness, they move over to the two sets of twins. All four designers are sitting beside each other and whispering.

"Girls," Hunter says, frowning, "it's completely possible that you both got dresses but—"

Jillian's face reddens as she interrupts Hunter. "We did both get dresses! I swear!"

"Fine, I'll give you the benefit of the doubt on that," Hunter says. "But I find it incredibly hard to believe that you both chose to make dresses with drawstring belts."

Rachel's face turns crimson. "We're twins. We have a sixth sense."

Jillian seems to sense things aren't going well. "We, um, also both chose Candy Land as our inspiration," she mumbles. "But it was total coincidence."

Luke laughs, but he's quickly silenced by Jasmine's killer stare. "This twinsy cuteness might have cut it if these designs were spectacular," she says. "Unfortunately, the beading and sequins look like a birthday cake exploded."

The girls' lips quiver at Jasmine's harsh words, and Jillian wipes at her eyes with the back of her hand. It's clear the sisters thought their designs were stellar.

Jasmine moves over to Sam and Shane, her lip curled in a sneer. I imagine the producers using a close up shot of that angry face for promos. "Do you and your brother have a sixth sense as well?" she asks sarcastically.

Shane looks shaken. "Sometimes, but not today," he says. He presents a pair of red corduroy pants. I'm not usually a huge fan of corduroy, but I have to admit the bold red makes them look cool and modern.

"I was inspired by the superhero section," Shane says. "Superheroes are clearly special, but they try to blend in among us. I thought about how I've been working to blend in here and tried to combine the elements of my home state of Texas with the originality of New York style."

Hunter, Missy, and Jasmine look at the pants from all sides. Finally Missy breaks the silence. "You didn't just try," she says, beaming, "you succeeded!"

Shane lets out an audible sigh, clearly relieved. Sam, on the other hand, is visibly sweating as he presents his denim vest. "I used the *Toy Story* section for inspiration since I love working with denim," he says, voice cracking. "I added leather fringe to the hem to give it a cowboy feel but kept the top simple and clean."

Even Jasmine seems to have pity for him. "Thank you, Sam. You can relax." She waves to one of the producers, and he brings over a cup of water, while another producer leans in for a close-up.

By the time the judges get to me, I just want to be done. It's been a long day. Hunter speaks first. "Chloe, I'm impressed. This skirt is not something I would have expected from you. The color and design both seem like a big departure from your usual style."

"They are," I agree. "I'm usually a bit more minimalist and drawn to neutral colors. But I was inspired to try something new this challenge."

Missy nods. "And what were you were inspired by?" she asks.

"The Ferris wheel," I say. Nina snorts, but I ignore her. "It reminded me of the fair that happens back home every summer. And one of my favorite things about the fair, aside from riding the Ferris wheel, is eating cotton candy, which is what helped inspire my skirt. I also spent some time in the store's Candy Land section, so that helped. I was going for a very whimsical feel, since that's what toy stores are really all about. I think the volume of the skirt and the scattered gems accomplish that."

"Very impressive," Hunter says. I smile, but the judges are already moving on to Daphne.

"What happened?" asks Missy, unable to control her surprise at Daphne's misshapen blouse.

Daphne throws her hands up helplessly. "The sewing machine and I had a fight. It won." She scrunches the pretty turquoise material in her hands as she talks. It's obvious how beautiful the blouse could have been.

The judges peer closely at the stitching. I'm sure there are good elements to Daphne's design, but the material looks so wrinkled and frayed, it's practically impossible to tell. There's nothing Daphne can do at this point, and she hangs her head in disappointment as the judges walk away to decide our fashion fate once again.

The judges are gone much longer than usual this time. I'm not sure if that's a good thing or a bad thing. Either they're having a hard time deciding between all the good designs, or they think everything was so bad it's impossible to choose. Finally, after almost an hour of deliberating, they reappear.

"Thank you for waiting," Jasmine says. "After much discussion, we have reached our decision. We thought having access to sewing machines this week would make things easier for you, but it seems we were wrong. Many of you struggled with this challenge. That's why this week we'll only have a top two, rather than a top five."

"Now on to the good news," Missy says, seeming eager to get things back on a more positive note. "Derek, it was a risky move to switch garments with Chloe, but it paid off for you. You're one of our top two designers this week."

Hunter steps forward with a smile. "It paid off for more than just you," he says. "We have a new addition joining the top of the pack today. Chloe, you really stepped outside your comfort zone and took this challenge to heart with your cotton-candy skirt. Well done. You're the other designer in the top two. Congratulations."

I can hardly believe what I'm hearing. I finally did it! "Thank you," I say gratefully. I want to scream and cheer and hug everyone around me, but we're not done. I have to be content with an excited grin.

"Of course with a top we must also have a bottom," says Hunter. "Luke, while we admire the ambition you showed in wanting to try something different, the short time frame doesn't leave time for any type of tie-dye. You clearly didn't plan well enough for your design, and therefore you're in the bottom five."

Luke's face falls as he drops a handful of soggy paper towels on the floor in front of his mannequin. I can't fault the judges for their critique — dye is still dripping off Luke's top.

"Joining him today is Daphne," Jasmine says. "I can certainly picture what the blouse could have been. The color was gorgeous, and I would have liked to have seen the finished product. Unfortunately, the sewing machine was your downfall today."

Daphne looks like she's trying not to cry as Jasmine turns to Rachel and Jillian. "Girls, not only were your designs almost identical — which is a blatant violation of the rules — they were lazy. It was clear you didn't give much, if any, thought to their execution. You're also in the bottom five."

"And rounding out our bottom five is Nina," Missy says. "We know you tried to show romance with your skirt, but I'm afraid the hearts along the hem came across as amateur. They didn't match the feel of the rest of the skirt and took away from the garment's sophistication."

I see Nina clench her fists. Clearly she thought her story about her first kiss would be enough to win over the judges.

"There's no need to draw this out," Hunter says. "Nina, Daphne, and Luke, you're safe today. Rachel and Jillian, it's clear you broke the rules by making identical designs. You will be leaving us today."

As Jillian and Rachel sniffle and start to say their goodbyes, Derek leans over and smiles at me. "Welcome to the top," he whispers. I can hardly believe it. My design has finally broken away from the middle of the pack.

Looks like Jake's advice paid off big time — making a connection was enough to propel me to the top.

30

"To your first big win," says Mom, raising her glass as we celebrate my success later that evening.

"Why thank you," I say, clinking glasses.

Mom smiles. "I'm glad you're in a better mood," she says. "Just remember that there are still several challenges left. I don't want one bad day making you doubt yourself, okay?" She tousles my hair like she did when I was little.

"Okay," I say. "I'll do my best."

Just then my phone buzzes. I look at the screen and see it's a text from Hunter. "You have got to be kidding me!" I exclaim. "We already had a challenge today." I push the phone away without reading his message.

"Maybe he's congratulating everyone for making it this far," Mom suggests.

I roll my eyes. "Doubtful." Sighing, I read his message aloud. "'Congratulations to all who've made it this far!'"

"See!" Mom says. "What did I tell you?"

"Don't say 'I told you so' yet," I warn her. "There's more."

I scroll down to read the rest of Hunter's text. "'The competition is getting fierce, and our next task is right around the corner. Literally. Meet us at ACE Hardware at eight o'clock sharp for the next challenge.'"

* * *

When I get to the hardware store around the corner from our hotel, something is off. It takes me a minute to realize what. Then it hits me — unlike before the other challenges, no one looks happy to be here. Except the judges maybe.

"I know none of you anticipated this next challenge so soon, but we like to keep you on your toes," Missy says. "After all, spontaneity is part of the fashion world."

"And ratings," someone mumbles.

Hunter grins. "Ratings are important for the show, but they also help you. In two challenges, we'll be down to the final five. In the next stages of the competition, having the opportunity to show your designs will be that much more important. The more the audience hears about and sees your designs, the better for you. Trust me."

The skin on my arms tingles. I think back to the *Design Diva* competitions Alex and I have watched. In past seasons, the final five had their designs displayed in Macy's and Saks store windows. One season, a challenge prize was a spread in *Vogue*. I would freak if I won something half that good.

"For today, all that matters is this elimination," Missy says. "You'll be divided into three teams. Two contestants from the losing team will be let go. This challenge will force you to think outside the box since you'll be using unique materials — duct tape or newspaper. You can use other supplies from the store as well, but one of those materials must make up the majority of your garment."

Around me, I hear the other designers grumbling. I don't blame them. I've seen some creative prom dresses made out of duct tape, but I certainly never expected to be working with the material myself. Let alone old newspaper.

"To keep things fair, your teams will be chosen randomly," Hunter says, passing around a basket full of folded slips of paper. "Everyone have a number? Good. All the ones stand by Jasmine. Twos, by Missy. Threes, to my right."

The designers shuffle to our designated places. My stomach drops as my group comes together: me, Nina, and Daphne. I'm not happy about it, but Nina and I have faked nice before. And if it means winning, I can do anything.

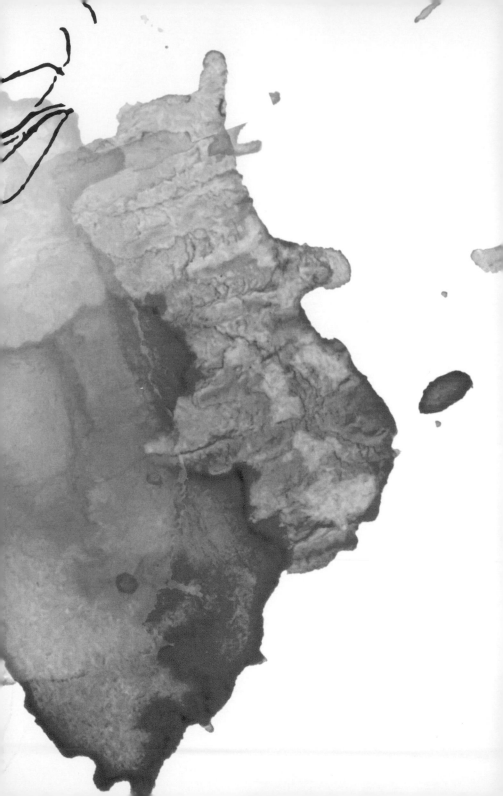

31

"You will have one hour to plan your design and gather materials and two hours to make it," says Hunter. "Decide as a group how you want to split up the duties. If it's best for each group member to work on his or her strength, that's fine. If you'd rather all work together, that's fine too. No aisle is off limits. You may begin."

Nina, Daphne, and I stare at each other for a moment. It's clear no one is quite sure where to begin. Then Daphne takes out her notebook and pencil. "Okay, let's get started. We need to figure out whether we're using tape or newspaper and figure out a design."

"Agreed," Nina says. "The bottom is not somewhere I want to be again."

"I vote for newspaper," I say. "It'll be easier to work with than duct tape. We could do a cool structured dress. Maybe with a pencil skirt or peplum or something. Or we could crinkle the paper to add volume and texture."

"I think we should add some color to it," Nina says. "Otherwise it's going to be too boring."

"We don't have time," I remind her. "Even if we could find the supplies to dye it, there's no time to let it dry. We'd be stuck with soaking wet newspaper. Remember what happened to Luke last challenge?"

Nina looks irritated, but Daphne nods. "Good point," she says. "Let's focus on making something really structural and detailed. That's a better use of our time."

"I disagree," Nina says.

"Well, this isn't the Nina group," Daphne replies.

Nina stares coldly at her. I've seen that look before, when one of her followers back home dared to disagree with her. The difference now is that Daphne doesn't back down. *Maybe she's someone to be reckoned with after all*, I think.

* * *

After twenty minutes of tossing our ideas around, we've managed to come up with a workable design — a structured, strapless dress with a pencil skirt and flared peplum. We split up to grab our materials — a huge stack of newspaper, some Velcro, white thread, straight pins, and several pencils, rulers, and pairs of scissors.

I grab three full-size sheets of newspaper and stack them together so all the edges are lined up. Starting at one side, I start to make pleats for the peplum, which will give our dress some visual interest and structural detailing. I use one of the rulers to measure and fold one side of the paper half an inch, then crease it to make sure it's crisp. Still moving from the same side, I make a one-inch fold, measuring carefully to make sure the pleats are straight. The bottom half of the dress depends on the structural details, so they have to be precise

Flipping the sheets of newspaper over, I fold the paper up to meet the edge of my original half-inch crease. Then I flip the newspapers over again, create another one-inch fold, and crease it firmly. In order to make the pleats, I have to create another smaller, half-inch crease, which I fold up to meet the edge of the first half-inch fold.

When I'm done, I glance down — one pleat done, about a million to go. Luckily, Daphne and Nina are already both hard at work pleating their own stacks of newspapers too. We need them for the peplum plus the waistband and back of the pencil skirt, so it's all hands on deck to get this skirt done in time.

Speaking of hands, I glance down at mine. They're covered in newsprint stains. *This is going to be a long, messy challenge*, I realize. *At least we talked Nina out of dyeing it.*

Once we have four sheets of pleats finished, it's time to start sewing. I measure to the center of two of the pleated pieces and draw a line in pencil to mark the spot. While I'm doing that, Nina measures the other two pieces and makes a mark about an inch and a half above the center point.

"We should baste them together first," Daphne says. "Or at least use a long stitch and a low thread tension. That way we can take the stitches out without ruining the paper if we need to."

"Good point," Nina agrees. "I don't want to have to redo all those pleats. And more importantly, we don't have time."

It's hard to believe Nina is being so agreeable. I glance at the other teams, and they seem to be working well together too. *Maybe we should have had partner tasks from the beginning*, I think. Not only are we getting way more done, but I'm much less anxious knowing we're doing this as a team — at least now that I see how well we're working.

Daphne moves over to the sewing machine and Nina and I exchange a nervous look. I can tell we're both remembering her losing battle with the sewing machine last challenge. Daphne must sense our fear, because she glances back at us. "Don't worry, I learned my lesson last time," she says. "I've got this."

Sure enough, Daphne sews straight across the pencil lines Nina and I drew, keeping the pleats properly folded as she moves the paper through the machine. Soon all four pieces have their pleats secured in place. Next Daphne grabs one of the pieces with the off-center stitching and lines up the seam with one of the center-stitched pieces, letting the pieces overlap about half an inch. She sews the two pieces together where they overlap, then does the same thing with the other two mismatched pieces. Finally, she sews the pieces together so we have a long strip of pleated paper.

Nina grabs a length of rope to use as a belt as we move over to our dress form to fit the newspaper bodice and peplum skirt. Daphne and I wrap the pleated paper around the dress form, making sure the center stitching hits at the natural waist. Then Nina belts it to hold it in place. The three of us exchange excited grins. It's really coming together.

I grab some pins to start fitting the bodice, pressing the pleats down across the chest so they lie close to the body. I pin the pleats in place in front and back, and Daphne grabs a pencil to trace the neckline and a deep, low-cut back. When we have the neckline set, we bring the bodice back over to the sewing machine and sew just below the traced line, pulling the pins out as we go.

Once we're finished stitching, we cut along the traced line to create the strapless neckline.

We add the Velcro closure at the back of the bodice and then sew a second waist seam to help smooth the pleats. Having two seams will make the midsection lie flatter and look more flattering. We put the bodice on our dress form for safekeeping. Now it's time to add the pencil skirt, which will be a separate piece.

I grab three sheets of newspaper, just like I did with the pleated peplum portion of the dress, and stack them on top of each other. I baste them together, then use an iron to smooth out any wrinkles. It's important for our pencil skirt to be sleek and straight in order to contrast with the flared peplum.

I sew as fast as I can, making sure to add a pleated center back vent to the bottom of the pencil skirt so the wearer can walk easily without tearing the dress. While I'm doing that, Nina and Daphne each make their own panels. Finally we connect all the bottom layers, sew them together near the top seams, and attach another piece of Velcro at the back.

"Thirty minutes!" Jasmine calls out.

Daphne, Nina, and I put the pencil skirt on the dress form and attach the pleated bodice and peplum over the top. Then we stand back to admire our work. The flared peplum stands out perfectly against the straight pencil skirt, and the neckline is perfectly fitted. But still . . .

"It needs something," Nina says. "It's too plain."

I study the dress too. I hate to admit it, but Nina is right. It does feel like it's still missing something.

Nina thinks for a minute, then snaps her fingers. "I've got it! A belt! I can make a thick one out of the pleated newspaper we have left to help define the waist."

I hear the gloating in Nina's voice. I know it's petty, but I hate that she's the one to come up with the idea. And I know she'll make sure everyone knows it.

Nina runs to grab more newspaper. I see her flipping through sheets of pleated paper until she finds what she's looking for — a section that's darker than all the rest.

"Fifteen minutes!" the judges announce.

Nina runs the belt through the machine quickly and attaches a piece of Velcro at the back. "Done!" she hollers triumphantly. She hurries back to the mannequin and adds the belt to our design.

I have to admit, it's perfect. The dark newspaper Nina chose is the perfect accent piece — it looks like a wide black belt cinching in the waist of the dress. There's no way one person could have gotten this much done in the time limit. This dress was truly a team effort. I can only hope it was a winning effort as well.

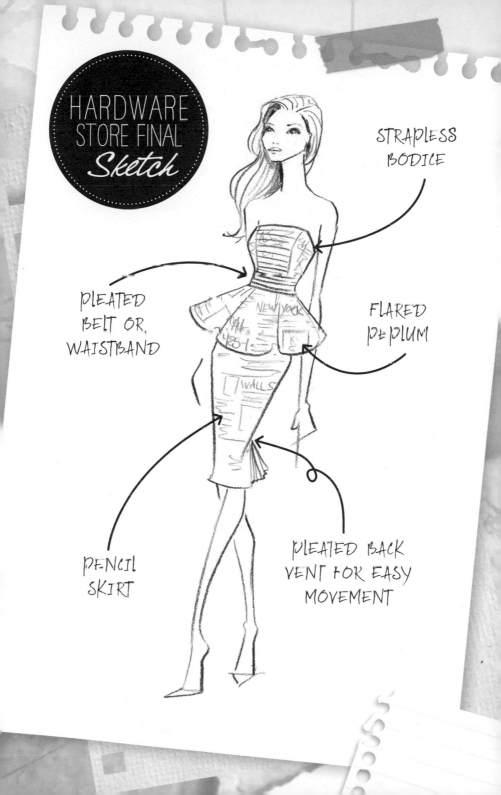

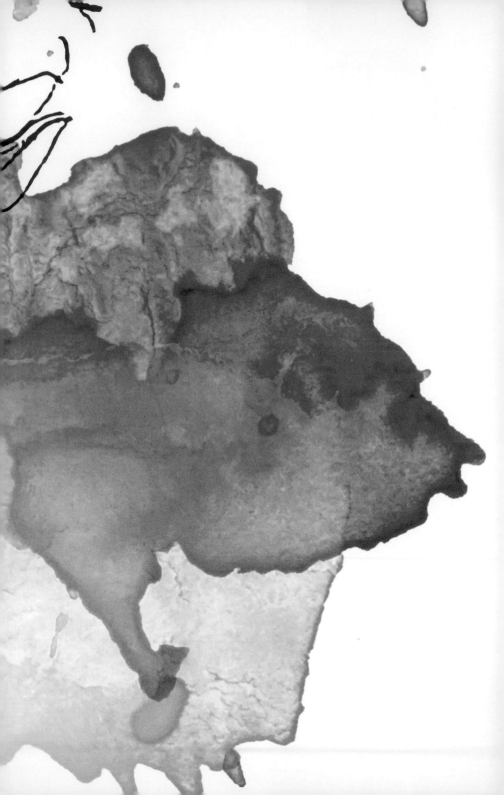

As the three teams assemble in front of the judges, I see that it's not just our group huddled together. Everyone seems to have bonded over this team task.

"First, let me say how impressed we are with the creativity of all the designs," says Hunter. "No one just slapped something together and called it art. You all made something unique and wearable out of unusual materials."

"I think I'd wear all these designs," Missy adds cheerfully.

"Let's start with group one," says Hunter, walking over to Derek, Luke, and Sam. They've created a high-low, A-line skirt with a chevron pattern entirely out of duct tape. "Great work, guys. I love the striking contrast

between the black and white, and the chevron pattern is very modern."

Jasmine moves around the dress form, examining the skirt from all angles. "It looks like you had some trouble in the back here. The lines don't seem to be as straight as they do on the front of the skirt. And they're a bit uneven."

"We had a little bit of difficulty getting the different sections measured precisely to line up our pattern," Derek says quietly.

"It was my fault," says Sam, looking at his feet. "I misjudged the pattern in the back."

"But we all came together to make it work and created a very wearable skirt," Luke says, trying to end on a positive note.

"Thank you," says Hunter. "Missy, do you want to discuss group two's design?"

"Love to!" Missy says, walking over to Shane, Curt, and Tom. They've created a dress with a full skirt made out of garbage bags and a strapless top out of black duct tape. Even from here, I can tell that it's not as sophisticated as group one's skirt.

We're the only group that went with newspaper, I realize. Hopefully that risk is a good thing. Maybe it will set us apart.

Missy examines the dress. "I like the look of this dress. The full skirt is very fun, and I like the varying proportions between that and the more fitted top. I could definitely see this as a party dress."

"Can I say something about it?" Jasmine asks. She doesn't wait for a response. "I appreciate the concept, but this skirt is seriously lacking in construction. It's all taped and scrunched; no sewing involved. And the skirt is really the focal point, not the duct-tape top. That'd be fine if the challenge hadn't been to use duct tape or newspaper for the majority of the garment."

"Curt made the skirt!" Tom mutters.

"What's your problem, dude?" says Curt. "You're the one who wanted to make the skirt out of trash bags."

Jasmine looks at Shane. "Well?" she says.

"Uh, yeah," Shane says, shooting his teammates an apologetic look. "It was Tom's idea, but Curt did most of the skirt construction."

"And where do you fit in here?" Jasmine asks.

"I, um, was in charge of the top," Shane says. "I wanted something fitted to contrast with the fullness of the skirt, and the black duct tape reminded me of patent leather, which is why I chose it."

Jasmine looks at him for a moment, and Shane seems to be holding his breath. "Good choice," she finally says.

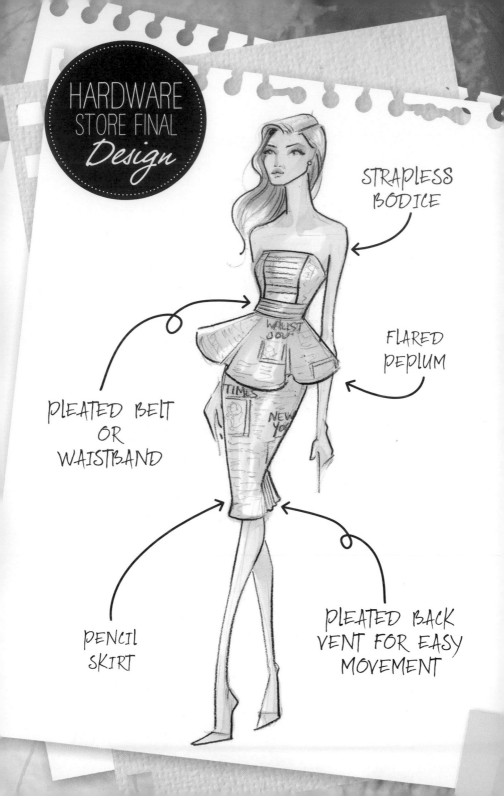

Shane lets out an audible sigh of relief as the judges move toward our group. Daphne, Nina, and I are still holding hands. My fingers are sweaty, but I don't let go.

"Girls, I have to say, I'm extremely impressed," Missy says. "You're the only group that chose to use newspaper for this challenge, and it really paid off. This dress is unique and beautiful."

"I agree," Hunter adds. "I'm glad to see one of the groups chose this material. It really lends itself well to the detail of your design."

Even Jasmine seems to be a fan. "I like the focus you've put on the natural waist of the dress," she says.

Nina is quick to speak up. "That was my idea," she says. "I thought the dress needed something to contrast the peplum and create added definition at the waist."

Knowing the cameras are on me, I have to fight the urge to roll my eyes. *Just keep smiling*, I think. *If we win, it won't matter that Nina took the credit. At least she didn't throw you under the bus.*

"Good choice," says Jasmine.

"I'm all about doing what's best for the team," Nina says, smiling sweetly. I grit my teeth at her fake team-player attitude.

Jasmine walks around the dress and examines the stitching and pleating. "Very nice," she finally says. "I have to say, I was not expecting this." Her face is serious, and I can't tell what she means. From the bewildered looks on Nina's and Daphne's faces, neither can they.

Finally the judges finish examining our dress and gather to deliberate.

"I think that went well," I whisper.

"We'll see," says Nina.

There's a lot of nodding and head shaking as the judges discuss the three designs. I try to read their lips, but Missy sees me looking and covers her mouth with her hand. Oh, well. I was never very good at lip-reading anyway.

"What do you think they're saying?" asks Daphne.

"That they've never seen anyone as talented as our group," I joke.

Nina snorts. "I wish."

I rub my eyes. Between the last challenge and this one, I'm exhausted. Today feels like it will never end. Finally, the judges seem to come to a decision.

Hunter walks over to the three groups again. "Thank you for your patience," he says. "We didn't want to make our decision in haste."

"You all did a fine job, but there was one group that exceeded our expectations," says Jasmine. "There were minor issues, but overall the design went above and beyond in terms of skill and creativity. Group three, congratulations. All three of you are safe tonight!"

Group three?! That's us! Nina, Daphne, and I all squeal and hug. But we don't have much time to celebrate. There's still an elimination to go.

"This means," Jasmine continues, "groups one and two, one of you is the bottom group. Tom, Shane, Curt, unfortunately, your dress just wasn't up to par tonight. The challenge was to use duct tape or newspaper, and you instead chose to focus on trash bags. What's more, your skirt construction was lacking. Tom and Curt, I'm sorry but you'll both be leaving us."

Tom and Curt shake hands with the judges and say their goodbyes to the other boys, who look sad to see them go. The seven of us who are still in the competition high-five happily. Nina, Daphne, and I laugh as we duck from the twins' fist bumps. When we get to the hotel, we say goodbye and head to our rooms.

I can't wait to crawl into bed. After tonight's challenge, I'll need my rest. After all, who knows what tomorrow will bring?

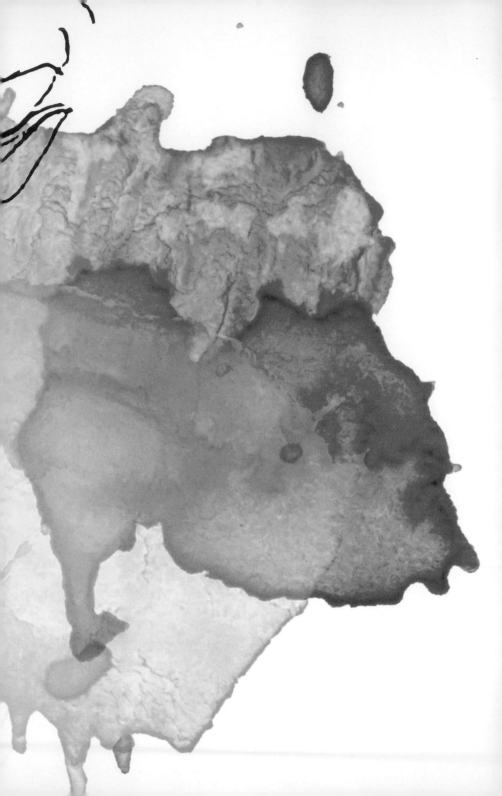

33

"Relax," my mom tells me as I bounce on the bed in our hotel room. It's been two days since the last challenge, and I'm still pumped up from my team's win.

"I'm trying to," I tell her. "I just can't take the suspense. We're supposed to meet today, and I still haven't heard any details." I turn on the television to distract myself, but the first thing I see is a promo for the next *Teen Design Diva* episode.

"Looks like they're airing the zoo challenge tonight," my mom says.

"I can't believe that was only two weeks ago," I say. "It feels like forever." My designs have certainly improved since then. Just then, my phone beeps with a text message, and I scramble to grab it. The text from the judges is short and sweet. "Lobby. Now."

* * *

When I get to the lobby, the judges are already there, standing by a large, opaque screen. As usual, they're surrounded by producers and cameras. One by one, the other designers arrive. There are only seven of us now, and we all have the same nervous look on our faces.

"It's good to see you all again," Missy says. "I hope you all used the past two days to rest up, because there are only three challenges left before we're down to the top three designers. That means the grand prize, an internship with a famous designer, is almost within reach. The next two weeks will be intense."

"And because of that, we've decided that for the next few tasks, you'll be getting some help," Hunter chimes in.

At his words, my fellow designers and I exchange confused looks. *What kind of help?* I wonder. Thankfully, the judges don't keep us in suspense for long.

"Our goal in this competition is to help you become stronger designers," Jasmine says. "What better way to do that than to learn from other success stories?"

My heart beats quickly. Who will be helping me?

"Ladies and gentlemen," Hunter says, "after careful screening of your skills and personalities, we have paired you with very willing mentors. Just to be clear, your mentor is not here to do your designs for you. That's your job. But their expertise will help you greatly. You should take advantage of their knowledge and experience."

"Especially because not too long ago, they were in your shoes," Missy adds. She points toward the nearby screen. "When the screen moves, you'll see your mentor on the other side holding a sign with your name."

With that, Jasmine waves her hand, and the screen drops. Standing behind it are contestants from past seasons of *Design Diva*. The cameras are poised to capture our reactions, but when I see who's holding my name, I'm so excited I almost forget all about filming. It's Liesel McKay!

"Liesel!" I exclaim. I can hardly believe my good luck. "I mean Ms. McKay."

"Liesel, please," she says with a smile as she walks toward me. "Ms. McKay makes me feel old."

"Is this okay?" I ask. "I mean, do the judges know we've met before?"

Liesel nods. "Yep, that's why they thought I'd make the perfect mentor for you," she says. "We already know each other! Ready to head out and discuss strategy?"

"Definitely!" I say. "Where to?"

Liesel walks toward the doors leading out of the hotel lobby. "We're headed to inspiration."

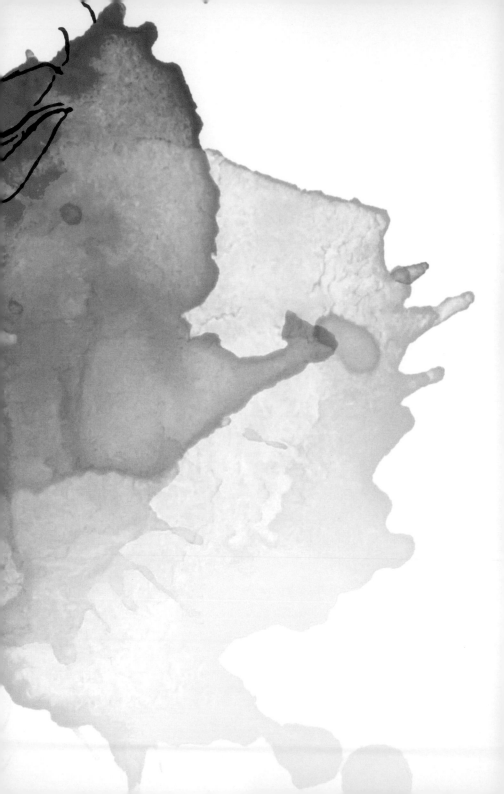

"I keep a notebook with me all the time," Liesel tells me as we stroll down the crowded sidewalk. "I write down everything. All my ideas and inspiration. You never know what might come in handy. I've woken up from dreams, jotted stuff down, and in the morning found 'banana peel' in my notebook. Then I spend all day trying to figure out what it means." She laughs.

"Do you always figure it out?" I ask.

"Not always, but it's worth writing down anyway," Liesel says. She lowers her voice to a whisper. "My biggest fear is running out of ideas. It's probably the biggest fear of most designers, honestly."

I can't believe that someone as successful as Liesel worries about running out of ideas. All of her clothes are so creative — and she makes jewelry and accessories on top of that. It seems like her creativity is never-ending.

"I have the opposite problem," I tell her. "The show gives us ideas. It's figuring out what to *do* with them that's hard."

"Some of them are really out there," Liesel agrees. "But you're definitely improving. You seem to be connecting with the work more."

I nod, thinking about what Jake said the other day. "I have Jake to thank for some of that," I admit. "I came by your store a few days ago, and that's the exact advice he gave me. Does he know you're my mentor?"

Liesel laughs. "Yes. It was impossible to keep it a secret from him. The producers made him sign papers swearing his life away if he breathed a word."

Well at least that's one person I won't have to keep things a secret from, I think.

"I can't wait until everyone knows everything," I tell Liesel. "I hate not being able to talk with Alex about the challenges. She's my best friend from back home. Not being able to tell her what's going on is torture!"

"I think I have something that will put you in a better mood," Liesel says with a secretive grin.

When I spot a giant sculpture of a needle threading a button, I suddenly realize where we are — the Garment District. It's been on my list of must-sees since I first watched *Design Diva*. High-profile designers walk these streets every day. I bet Liesel knew coming here would provide the inspiration I need.

In minutes, we're standing in front of the fabric store to end all fabric stores. Liesel certainly meant what she said about having something to put me in a better *mood*. The sign in the window says it all — Mood Designer Fabrics.

I can't believe I'm actually here. I whip out my phone, snap a photo of the store entrance, and send it to Alex. That's not breaking the rules. After all, I could be here on my own, regardless of the competition.

"Shall we?" Liesel says. She holds the door open for me, and I follow her into the elevator.

"Mood?" the elevator operator says knowingly. Liesel nods and he pushes the button for the third floor.

Minutes later the doors open, and I'm transported to heaven. There are rows of fabric in every type of material, print, and color imaginable. Mannequins wearing designs are posed around the store, and there are buttons, accessories, and thread everywhere. It's like I'm in a design sanctuary. I don't know where to go first.

Liesel seems to sense how overwhelmed I am. "I could so easily go bankrupt in here," she says. "Promise me you won't let me spend more than a hundred dollars today."

"I'll try," I say. It's a good thing we're not allowed to bring own materials to challenges, or I'd be working off my debt for the rest of life. For today, I'll just browse. When the show is over I can come back and stock up.

"Follow me," says Liesel. "And pay attention."

It's hard to know what Liesel has in mind, so I try to take in everything. Swatch, the adorable bulldog and unofficial store mascot I've seen on *Design Diva*, sits on the carpet. Beside him, college students sift through earring pieces. Behind them, two elderly men measure out yards of fabric. Two punk-looking guys and two women in business suits flip through bolts of plaid fabric, while a Girl Scout troop examines hair accessories.

Liesel stops. "So what do you think?"

About what? I think. "I'm sorry," I say, feeling like I've failed. "I don't understand the question. What should I have been looking at?"

Liesel smiles. "Everything."

Oh, great. That clears it up. "Um . . . there was a lot to see," I say slowly.

Liesel studies me. "You mean you didn't notice the uniformity among the customers? You missed the pattern?"

Darn it! I knew this place was over my head. Should I make something up? No. Better to go with the truth. I don't want to embarrass myself any more than I already have.

"No," I admit, avoiding Liesel's gaze. "I didn't."

Liesel claps her hands. "Great!"

"Excuse me?" I say, feeling like Clueless Chloe.

"There is no pattern," Liesel says, grinning. "That's the point. There are all sorts of people here. You might think you know what they're going to like, but you'd be wrong. Try thinking outside the box. Take an idea and run with it, even if you're not sure it's what the judges want. Because you know what?"

"What?" I ask.

"Even they don't know what they want!" Liesel says. "The lack of pattern and uniformity is what makes fashion so fun. No two designers are the same. Even if everyone uses the same materials, the end results will be unique."

I nod. Liesel's advice sounds like what my mom said about Nina stealing my ideas — what she does doesn't affect me. I'm my own designer.

"There's more than one way to make a connection," Liesel says. "Know your design aesthetic and go from there. But don't be afraid to let some other inspiration in and think outside the box."

Liesel and I spend the next two hours wandering the aisles, discussing fabrics and designs. She shows me color combinations I would have never thought of, and I take notes on design techniques. By the time I get a text about the next challenge, Liesel has spent $99.99, and I've managed to accumulate some priceless information.

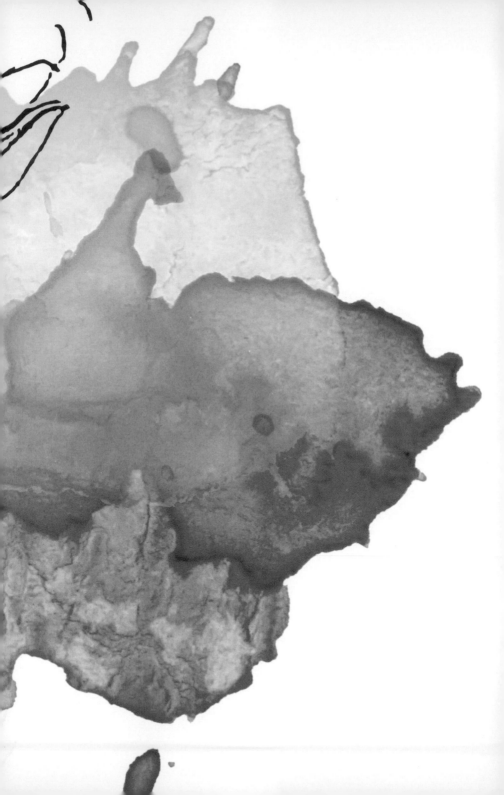

35

The next morning, the remaining designers are up bright and early. Our next challenge starts at 7:30 a.m. at the Sony Wonder Technology Lab, and no one wants to be late. At least this time we're not facing the judges alone. Our mentors are standing there beside us, and a giant, three-stories-tall, inflatable Spiderman clings to the glass above where we're standing.

"Welcome to the Sony Wonder Technology Lab," Hunter says when everyone has gathered. "I think you'll really enjoy today's challenge."

Behind me, I hear one of the other designers snort. I can understand the skepticism. I might be excited and energized after my visit to Mood yesterday, but to say we'll "enjoy" a challenge is pushing it. Challenges are a new kind of high-level stress.

Hunter chooses to ignore the snort. "As you can see, Missy and Jasmine aren't here today," he continues. "Instead, we'll be joined by two guest judges: Carmine Franklin and Jerome Grubin. You may not recognize their names, but I'm sure you know their work. Both Carmine and Jerome have been instrumental in the design of world-building games: *Choose Your Destiny* and *It's All Up to You*."

No way! Those are the most amazing video games ever. They let you create a future life, from career to clothing to the entire city you live in. I always make myself a fashion designer, and I'm betting the other six contestants do the same.

"Now that we're down to seven contestants, there will be no top and bottom five," Hunter tells us. "Instead, we will have two top spots, two middle, and three bottom. And only one person will be eliminated this round. Make sense?"

Everyone nods in understanding, and Hunter grins. "Great. That brings me to today's good news," he continues. "From here on out, there will also be a winner for each challenge. For this challenge, the prize for the best design will be the opportunity to work with both Carmine and Jerome to create a line of clothing for avatars to wear."

All around me, the other designers gasp with excitement. I'm right there with them. Imagine players throughout the world choosing my designs for their avatars! It's almost too good to be true.

Hunter laughs. "So now do you believe me about this challenge being fun? You'll have two hours to explore the lab with your mentor. Find an exhibit that speaks to you. When you're done, you'll have another two hours to design and create something that showcases the essence of this museum. Got it? Good. Your time starts now."

Liesel and I immediately head for the glass elevator, which looks like something out of a science-fiction movie. We take it up to the fourth floor, and as soon as we step off I see a Sensitile exhibit. We touch the wall, and the special material it's made of creates unique reflections in response to our touch.

I overhear a guide talking to a group of people. "Everything you do here," she's saying, "creates an impact on the lab and one another."

I file that away for a possible design theme, then walk with Liesel to get our ID cards. Nothing is ordinary here. For the cards, we type our names, choose a color and music genre we like, take our picture, and record our voices. Our digital profiles will be used to help personalize our experience.

Once we have our personalized ID cards, Liesel and I move on. We stop at something called The Robot Zone, which lets visitors program one of six colored robots, each equipped with light and touch sensors. Derek and his mentor are already there. I choose a blue robot, Liesel chooses yellow, and we direct our robots around the circle. The sensors determine how the robots will act.

"I think our robots like each other," I say as Liesel's yellow guy follows my blue one around.

"I think mine likes both of yours," Derek says as his red robot gets in on the action. We watch the three robots interact and scoot around the circle.

"Are there enough for us?" a snippy voice asks from behind me. I turn and see Nina and her mentor, Tanya Heartly, designer of Heart Jeans, standing behind us. Nina looks irritated, as if I've already told her she's not allowed to play with us.

"Sure," I say, and Nina picks a green robot. Her robot circles the ring, trying to interact with the others. It does fine with Derek's robot, but when it moves closer to mine, the blue robot quickly scoots away.

I want to laugh, but Nina looks angry. "Hey," I say, "I can't control what it does. They decide how to interact on their own."

"Whatever," Nina mutters.

"You don't need them," her mentor says. "Let's go." With that, the two of them leave to check out the other exhibits.

"I didn't do that on purpose," I say.

"Don't worry about it," Liesel says, shaking her head. "She and Tanya seem to be a good fit."

"Yeah? What's Tanya like?" I ask. "Did you spend much time with her on your season?"

Liesel shrugs. "I tried to avoid her for the most part because she doesn't have a good energy. She can be pretty cutthroat, which is kind of ironic considering the name of her brand. During our season, she sabotaged some of the other designers. She never admitted it, but we knew it was her."

Would Nina do that? I wonder. I'd think she'd want to win honestly, but who knows. I push thoughts of Nina out of my head and follow Liesel to the Interactive Floor. There we stand on circles of colored light that expand and contract as we move. The more we move, the more the circles interact. I walk my pink circle over to Liesel's green one and connect them. Soon Daphne joins us and walks her circle over as well. All our colors are connected, and it looks like a pyramid. I snap a picture with my phone — maybe that'll serve as inspiration later.

"How much time is left?" I ask Liesel.

"About an hour. You should probably start thinking about the direction you want to take your designs," she suggests.

I've been thinking about it since we walked in. I scan the remaining exhibit summaries to find one that will mesh with the idea I have brewing. "Let's go to the Shadow Garden and Sand Interactive," I say.

Liesel fake bows to me. "Your wish is my command," she says.

I glance across the room and spot Nina and Tanya looking at us. Nina whispers something to Tanya, and they both laugh. I turn away.

"Don't let them get inside your head," says Liesel. "Focus on your design."

"You're right," I say, smiling as we walk to the Shadow Garden.

The exhibit is crowded with people when we arrive. Cascading colored sand reacts to the shadows projected on the wall. I get in on the action, watching the sand accumulate based on the shapes my shadow creates. When I dance, the sand forms a line. When I move my right arm, the sand follows. I spread my arms wide, and the sand splits in two. The more our shapes change, the more sand accumulates. I watch someone step away from the wall, and the sand design he made falls.

I think about all the exhibits I've seen today. One robot's actions affected how another behaved. The colored circles only stayed in place if Liesel, Daphne, and I were all there. And the sand only worked if someone was there to engage it. In one way or another, each exhibit was influenced by the environment around it.

Interactivity, that's my inspiration. Now I just have to figure out how to turn that idea into an outfit that's wearable — and winning.

SONY
TECH LAB
Sketches

My ideas!!

EXHIBITS
VISITED

- SHADOW GARDEN
- INTERACTIVE FLOOR
- ROBOT ZONE
- SENSITILE

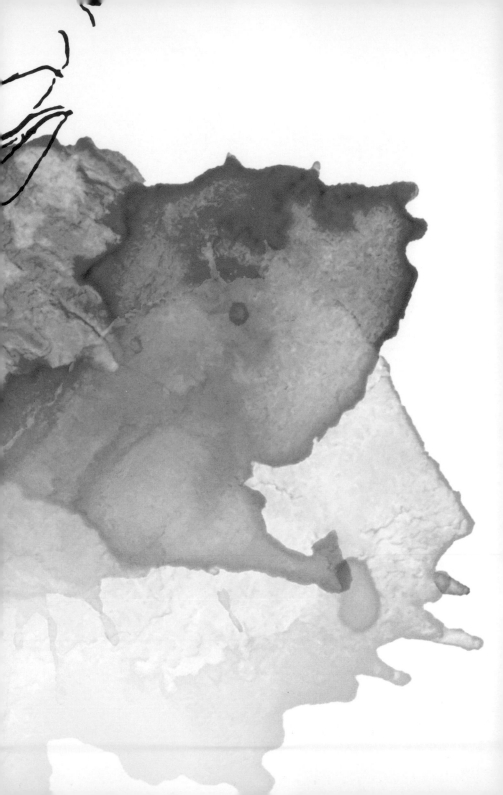

When our two hours of exploration are up, we all gather back at the entrance. Hunter leads us into a room filled with tables, sewing machines, and fabrics. Today's bookshelf is overflowing with different fabrics.

"Designers, you'll have two hours to complete your designs," Hunter reminds us. "Your mentors are here to oversee your designs and offer advice, but you must do all designing and garment construction on your own. Are we clear?"

All the designers and mentors nod in agreement. I'm already mentally sketching my idea and envisioning my materials so I can get started as soon as Hunter gives us the go-ahead.

"And remember," Hunter tells us, "your design should be inspired by something you saw here today. Ready? Go!"

Right away I spot a bolt of silver crepe on a rack off to the side. I reach out and feel the soft material with my hand. This silky, flowy fabric is exactly what I need. The way it moves and flows reminds me of how the sand moved with my body in the Shadow Garden and Sand Interactive.

On a nearby rack, I spot a bolt of mirrored, metallic fabric. Jackpot! That will be the perfect accent. And even better, the contrast between the materials — light and dark — is reminiscent of the contrast my shadow created when it was projected against the wall.

I grab the mirrored fabric, hold it up against the silver, and admire the combination. "What do you think?" I ask Liesel.

Liesel eyes the metallic material I picked. "I love the contrast," she says. "How are you planning on putting them together?"

"I'm going to use the crepe for the majority of the dress because it moves so well," I explain. "I was thinking of doing something with one shoulder and maybe adding a loose, flowy sleeve. And then I want to use the mirrored fabric at the waist to add shape and definition. It will look almost like a cut-out."

I hold the pieces up against the mannequin as I explain my vision, and Liesel nods. "The mirrored inset

will help add some structure to the looser fabric, too, which I love," she says. "Seems like you have it all figured out. But how does your design fit into the challenge? What's the connection to the exhibits we saw?"

I alternate between working and talking. I have too much measuring, cutting, and stitching to do to stop and chat for long. "The way the material falls reminds me of the sand in the Shadow Garden," I explain. "Whenever someone walked away, it sort of cascaded to the ground. And the reflective material is there to represent my biggest takeaway — that all the exhibits we saw today were reflections of their environment."

Liesel nods. "You're really on to something, Chloe. I might have to carry your stuff in my store after all this is over." She winks at me.

A design with Liesel? I'm definitely dreaming. But if I want that dream to come true, I'd better get to work. I drape the silver crepe across my dress form, trying to work with the flow of the material. I don't want the dress to look sloppy, so I need the top to be fitted enough to balance out the looser, knee-length skirt I have planned.

"One hour!" yells Hunter.

Next I grab the mirrored fabric I'll be using at the waist of my dress. I measure it against the mannequin and start cutting. So far so good.

I finish measuring and race over to the sewing machine. Thank goodness we have access to them now. Sewing by hand would make this challenge almost impossible. I pin the mirrored material to the silver fabric and use my marking chalk to keep track of where to attach it. I'm comfortable with sewing these pieces together. The stitching reminds me of attaching the faux leather panels in some of my earlier designs.

"Thirty minutes," calls Hunter. "Thirty minutes!"

I think about what Liesel told me in Mood about there being more than one way to make a connection. I was always so worried about switching things up that I didn't focus on what I did best. It's completely possible to use similar techniques from one design to the next and still produce a fresh, new product.

I add a side zipper to my dress and carry the nearly finished garment back over to the dress form to make sure it fits. Once I'm satisfied with the tailoring, I grab a steamer to use the final few minutes to get rid of the wrinkles in the material. In earlier tasks, I might have panicked and settled for good enough, but not today. I want this design to be perfect.

"And time," says Hunter. "Hands up."

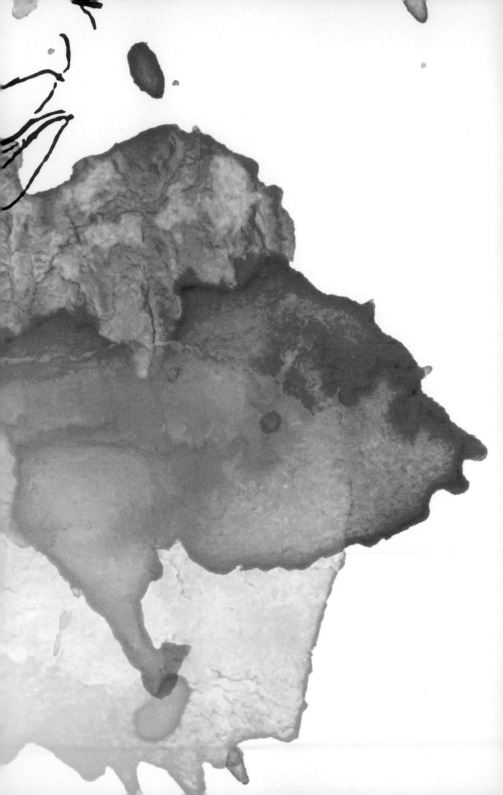

When it's time for the judging to start, I stand nervously beside my dress and wait. Hunter and the two guest judges, Carmine and Jerome, walk from design to design, finally stopping at Daphne's structural fluorescent green top and metallic skirt.

"Here's what I like," says Jerome. "Your bold color choices show you're not afraid to take risks. That's important in the design world." Daphne beams happily. Neon isn't my style, but clearly Jerome feels differently.

"The problem, though," Jerome continues, "is this silver, crinkly material you chose for the skirt. What is it?"

"Mylar," says Daphne quietly.

"Like what balloons are made of?" Carmine asks.

Daphne nods. "My theme was 'Wave of the Future.' That's what the museum represented to me." Her voice shakes. If Missy were here, she'd jump to comfort Daphne.

"Hmmm," says Jerome, checking the stitching. "Thank you, Daphne."

Luke is up next. His mannequin is wearing a metallic dress with sequins and studs on the exaggerated shoulders.

"I see someone else was going for the look of the future, too," Hunter comments.

"That's right," says Luke. "I used metallic fabric and added to the shine with studs and sequins."

Carmine feels the pointy studs Luke used to embellish the shoulders of his dress. She smiles. "I'm not sure studded shoulder pads are my style, but your perspective is very clear. I have to commend you for that."

Luke's smile doesn't waver. "To each his own, right?"

"Gotta stay true to your vision," Hunter agrees. He moves on to Derek, whose design, as usual, is flawless. "Tell us about your design, Derek. What inspired it?"

"It's called 'Behind the Seams,'" Derek says. "I was inspired by the animation exhibit. Usually, what happens behind the scenes of technology is a mystery. But here, when I made my own animation, I got to see how it worked."

"So how does that play into your design?" Carmine asks.

Derek turns the skirt inside out and reveals hidden pockets sewn inside. "I added interior pockets to this high-low skirt," he explains. "They're hidden but still useful."

OTHER CONTESTANTS' *Designs*

DAPHNE'S DRESS
WITH BUBBLE SKIRT

LUKE'S DRESS
WITH EXAGGERATED SHOULDERS

DEREK'S DRESS
WITH HIGH-LOW SKIRT

Carmine looks impressed. "You took the idea and ran with it." She returns the skirt to its correct side. "You can't even see where the pockets were sewn in. Your stitching and garment construction are flawless."

The judges move on to the next designer, Nina.

"Nina, what do we have here?" Hunter asks.

Nina squares her shoulders and gives the judges a wide smile. "I made a dress-and-headband combo, and I call it 'Silent Voices.'" She stares at the judges expectantly like they're supposed to know what she means by that.

Hunter clears his throat. "Well, uh, how about you explain how that theme works with your pieces."

Nina keeps smiling and shows off the taffeta dress she's made. "I incorporated the same material into her oversized hair bow," she says. "The material is noisy, but that's the irony. Technology may make a lot of noise, but it's, like, the uh, unrecognized parts of our world."

Huh? I think. The judges look confused too, and I spot Tanya shaking her head. Nina shoots her a confused look. I bet Tanya told Nina what to say, and she flubbed it.

"You're right; there is a lot about technology that we don't know," Hunter says, clearly trying to throw Nina a bone. "Thanks for sharing."

Then it's my turn. Liesel squeezes my shoulder as the judges approach. Before they can even ask what inspired me, I blurt out, "I was inspired by the different interactive exhibits and how they reflected their environments."

Jerome laughs a little at my obvious enthusiasm, and Carmine and Hunter study the dress's construction.

"I like your choice of materials," Jerome says. "The mirrored panel at the waist is the perfect contrast to the rest of the dress in terms of both structure and material."

Carmine nods. "I agree. Can you tell us more about why you chose these two fabrics in particular?"

I take a deep breath. "As I said, I was inspired by the interactive exhibits, particularly the Shadow Garden and Sand Interactive," I begin, motioning to my dress. "I chose this silver crepe because there's real movement in the material. The way it falls and waves reminds me of how the sand cascaded to the ground when someone stepped away from the sand wall. Plus the contrast between the light crepe and the darker mirrored panel reminds me of how shadows are created in the first place."

Hunter nods and smiles, and I take it as a signal to keep going. "All the exhibits we visited today were reflections of their environment and the people interacting with them," I continue. "Nothing could exist alone. No matter what, the exhibits all reflected how we interacted with them. This reflective material I used at the waist is a literal representation of that concept."

Hunter nods again. "Well put, Chloe," he says.

The judges move on to Sam's and Shane's designs, and I hear them asking Sam a lot of questions about his choice of material and stitching technique. Hunter seems to be examining his design closely, but I can't hear what exactly he's saying. Sam always seems to come out on top, though, so I bet he's not worried.

When they're finished examining the last design, the judges move to stand in front of the row of designers. "I can see you all took this challenge very seriously," Hunter says. "Must have something to do with the great prize. Once we've finished deliberating, we'll let you know who the lucky winner is and who will be going home."

With that, the judges leave the room, and all we can do is sit and wait. Sam and Shane are deep in whispered discussion. Daphne is staring off into space, Luke looks lonely, and Nina looks annoyed. Only Derek appears relaxed, leaning back with his hands behind his head.

After about thirty minutes, the judges reappear. Everyone immediately perks back up and pays attention.

"Let's start with our favorite designs of the day," Carmine says. "Chloe and Derek, you both impressed us with your thematic application and use of fabric. We also like how you both expanded your thinking in terms of what this challenge required."

Derek and I exchange happy grins. I'm so excited and relieved, I could burst. But the judges aren't finished.

"Now on to the not-so-good news," Jerome says. "While we did like everyone's attempt to convey a message through his or her designs, it seems like a few of you lost something in the execution. Daphne, your colors were daring, but we can't get on board with wearing Mylar. It just didn't work."

Daphne nods, but she looks like she might cry. I think of how put together she was during the team challenge at the hardware store and feel bad for her.

"Luke," Carmine says, "while I really admire how you stuck to your guns in terms of your very modern vision, I can't see anyone off the runway wearing studded shoulder pads. I'm sorry."

Hunter speaks up next. "The last person joining the bottom three today is Nina. You may have had an interesting design, but we didn't understand your concept. And unfortunately, I don't think you did either."

Nina looks up in horror. She clearly wasn't expecting to be in the bottom today.

"Sam and Shane, you're both safe for today," says Hunter. "Unfortunately, one of our bottom three will be eliminated today. Nina, although your point of view was confusing, we were able to see beyond that to what the design could be. Daphne, while we didn't like the Mylar, we liked the choice of color. Luke, I'm sorry but there were too many things that did not work for us with your piece. It just wasn't wearable, and there was no clear connection to the challenge. You'll be leaving us today."

Surprisingly, Luke takes the elimination well. "Thank you all for this opportunity," he says. "It's been a great experience. I promise you'll see me again."

"I have no doubt about that," Hunter agrees. "In fact, I look forward to it."

"Shall we end this with some good news?" asks Carmine.

"What would that be?" Jerome teases. "Oh, yes, the big winner." He pauses for effect, and my hearts pounds with anticipation. "Derek and Chloe, we really enjoyed both of your designs. However, one of them really stood out. Chloe, both your theme and execution captured the essence of this task. Congratulations! Your designs will be featured in video games worldwide!"

I can't believe it! Did he really just say my name? I think. I must not be imagining things, because in seconds Liesel is hugging me. The rest of the contestants congratulate me too. Everyone except for Nina.

I catch her looking at me and can't help but think that if looks could kill, I'd be in serious trouble.

The next morning, loud shouting wakes me up from a deep sleep. I'm confused for a second. *Where am I?* I think, looking around through half-closed eyes. Not my room at home — the hotel. In New York. As soon as my mind clears, I jump up and run to my phone, worried I've missed a message about an upcoming challenge.

"What time is it?" my mom asks groggily.

I look at the time on my phone. "Six a.m.," I tell her. No text from Hunter, thank goodness. But the shouting is getting louder. I open the door a crack and see Sam standing in the hallway. The door to his room is open, and Shane is standing beside it. Both of them look devastated.

"How could you do this?" Shane shouts at his twin.

"I panicked!" Sam yells. "I wanted to win."

"But you were doing fine," Shane says. "Now they're going to think I'm a cheater too."

"It was just some thread and a piece of fabric. It's not a big deal," Sam insists.

What thread? What fabric? I think. My groggy six a.m. brain is not putting the clues together fast enough.

"It *is* a big deal," Shane says. His voice is quieter now but just as angry. "We can't bring any of our own materials to the challenges. You knew that! Did you think the judges wouldn't notice?"

Suddenly what they're talking about makes sense. Sam must have somehow brought his own materials to the challenge yesterday. Hunter's excessive questioning about Sam's stitching and choice of material makes sense now too. He must have suspected something was up when the material wasn't one he recognized.

"I'm sorry," Sam says. "I'm really sorry."

"Well, sorry isn't going to cut it since you've been disqualified," Shane says. "We were going to do this together. And you ruined it."

I close the door and slump back on the bed, too awake to go back to sleep. "It sounds like Sam was eliminated," I tell my mom. "He cheated."

Mom shakes her head. "Pressure gets to people," she says.

I nod but don't say anything. With Sam gone we're down to five designers, but this is not how I thought the next elimination would go.

* * *

A few hours later, I head down to the lobby to find some breakfast. I must not have been the only one awoken by the twins' early morning shouting match, because the other designers are downstairs too. I grab a croissant and some juice from the buffet and sit beside Daphne.

"Crazy morning, huh?" she says.

"Yeah, no kidding," I agree, taking a bite of pastry. "So Sam is really gone? For good?"

Daphne nods. "That's what it sounds like. I guess Hunter talked to him this morning after he confirmed Sam used his own material during the last challenge."

"Jeez," I say, looking down. There are cameras stationed around the breakfast area, and I'm sure they're hoping to catch some of the drama for the show.

"The thing is . . . I can understand why he did it," Daphne says. "I mean, I'm not saying it was right. But it's easy to lose yourself and just see the finish line, you know?"

I nod. It is easy to get caught up in wanting to win, but deep down, I know I'd never cheat. If I cheated to get to the top, how would I know if I have what it takes?

"I'll be honest, I thought about it," Daphne confesses. "When we had time off, I went to Mood and bought some fabric and a few accessories. I didn't buy them so I could use them to cheat. I wanted them for my own projects when I get back home. But before this happened with Sam, I kind of wondered if anyone would really notice if I snuck some in."

"But you decided not to use them," I say. "That's what's important."

Daphne shrugs. "I guess. I hate that I thought about it at all, though."

"Don't be so hard on yourself," I say, patting Daphne's arm. "This competition makes it really easy to doubt yourself."

Daphne sniffles. "You didn't."

I take a deep breath. I really don't want to get into all my self-doubt, especially in front of the cameras. But I'm not perfect, and I don't need people thinking I am. "That's not true," I tell her. "I've doubted myself plenty. Especially at the beginning. I couldn't figure out what I needed to do to make it to the top. I thought maybe my designs weren't good enough and that my being here was a mistake."

Daphne looks surprised. "But you always seem so put together."

I laugh in disbelief. *Put together? Me? I never thought I'd hear those words.* "Can you put that in writing, please? I never feel that way."

"Everyone thinks so," Daphne says. I must look nervous, because she quickly adds, "Not that we talk about you. Just, you know, after the past few wins, Derek, Shane, and I were saying you're the one to beat."

I'm the big competition? I can hardly believe what I'm hearing. I guess I was so busy focusing on my own flaws that I didn't take the time to realize everyone else is scared too. Daphne and I sit quietly for a few minutes. Suddenly, our phones buzz at the same time. That can only mean one thing — a new challenge.

Daphne looks at her screen. "The judges want to see everyone downstairs in an hour."

"Fantastic," I say. "Better go shower and make myself look presentable."

"Same here," says Daphne. "And, hey, thanks for listening."

"Anytime," I say. "It's nice to have someone to talk to here. And you made the right choice."

"I'll keep telling myself that," says Daphne. "Even if I lose, at least I will have lost fairly, right?"

I grin. "Right. But we won't lose."

Daphne smiles ruefully. "That's a nice thought, Chloe, but somebody has to."

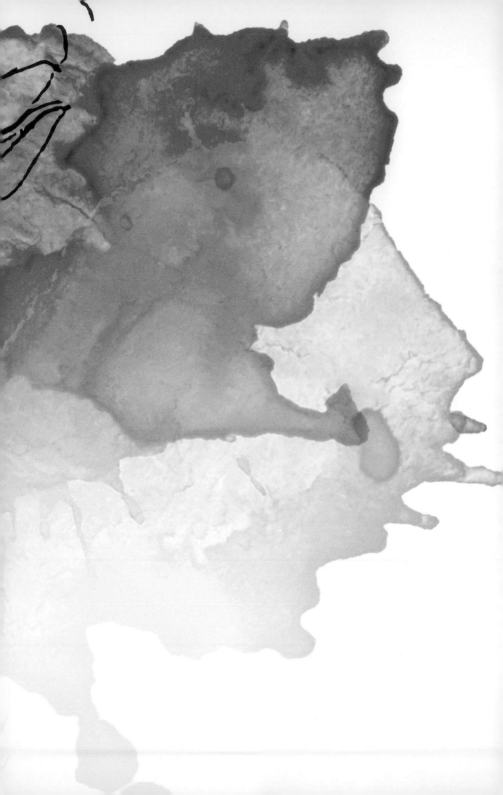

An hour later, all the designers are back in the lobby. This time, the regular judges   Hunter, Missy, and Jasmine — are all there too.

"By now I'm sure you've all heard about what happened with Sam," Missy says. "Because of that, Sam will no longer be with us."

I glance over at Shane to see how he's holding up without his twin here. It's hard to tell, though. The whole time Missy speaks, Shane stares at the floor.

"I'd like to say this has never happened before, but honestly, I can't," Jasmine says. "We realize that this is a high-pressure competition, and sometimes that gets to people. You're all young, and this is a learning experience. So let's do this last leg right. Believe in

315

yourselves. You wouldn't be here if we didn't believe in you."

"Unfortunately, Sam's disqualification from the competition has forced us to alter our elimination schedule," Hunter chimes in apologetically. "The good news is that means we'll be giving you the rest of the week off so we can regroup and adjust the schedule. The bad news is there's now only one challenge left before we're down to the final three."

"That's it?" Daphne cries. She looks a little frantic. "But why not have two challenges and eliminate one person in each?"

Hunter looks sympathetic. "That was the plan, but in light of recent events, we decided it was a better idea to give you more time in the final task. We'll have another challenge next week, after which two designers will be eliminated. The remaining three will go on to the final challenge and compete for the grand prize — an internship with a world-class designer. For the final challenge, you will be permitted to use one of your own items. We'll air the results live the following week."

Around me, the remaining designers look worried. I don't blame them. There are only five of us left — me, Nina, Daphne, Derek, and Shane — and this is a lot of information to take in at once. Instead of two more challenges to prove ourselves, we only have one. Hunter sounded like he wanted to take some of the pressure off, but all this has done is add more.

I try to remember Liesel's advice about staying positive and what Jake said about making a connection with the tasks. *I've made it this far*, I think. *What's one more challenge?* I look at the camera guys and give them what I hope looks like a winning smile.

Take that, pressure.

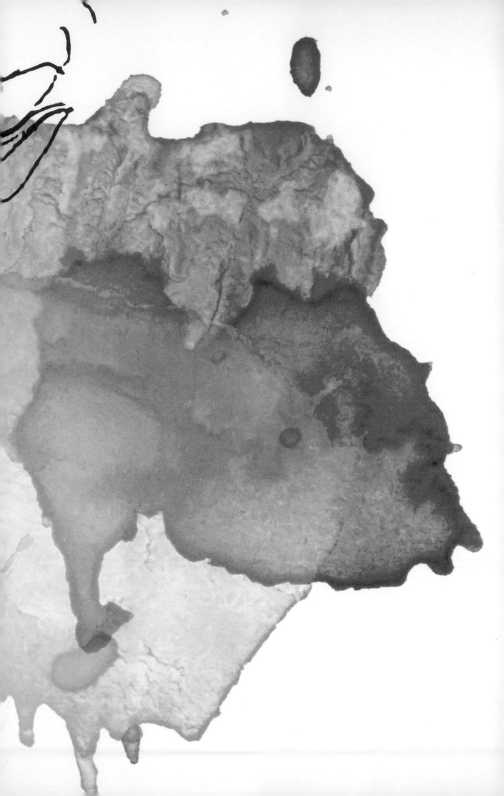

Sunday night I dream of dresses. They come out of closets and drawers, one by one. I'm trapped in a sea of pastels, sequins, and lace as the dresses march in a parade all their own. A taffeta gown sails over my head and shiny crinoline joins it. Some have tacky sashes, others V-necks and open backs. They lead me to a room packed with party dresses. There's no room to stand or sit, so I squeeze myself into a corner while the dresses dance.

My sketchpad appears, and I make notes about the dresses, but suddenly Jasmine whisks it out of my hand. "The task starts now!" she says.

My breathing quickens as I try to grab materials and scissors, but all the other designers are there too, and they get to them first.

"Keep up the pace!" Hunter yells.

Out of nowhere, Missy calls time and rings a bell.

I jolt awake, sweaty with panic, still hearing the bell. I try to clear my head, but the bell rings and rings. Suddenly I realize where the noise is coming from — my phone. I reach for it, groggy and confused, and read the text. I have to be in the lobby in one hour to start the next challenge.

With a groan, I pull the pillow over my head and try to collect my thoughts, but the parade of dresses keeps flashing behind my closed eyes.

* * *

When I get downstairs, it's like my dress dream has come to life. In the lobby, I see rack after rack of party dresses and fancy suits. But they're not fabulous by any means — they're hideous. Most of them are styles I've only seen in ancient fashion magazines or eighties movies. I pinch myself to make sure I'm not still dreaming. Ouch! Definitely awake.

"Welcome to your next challenge," Jasmine says. "As you know, today's task will determine who makes it to the final three. Because of the complexity of this assignment, you'll be allowed to consult with your mentors. And you'll have the whole day — a total of six hours — to complete your designs."

I get Liesel and a whole day to design and sew? I think. *What could possibly be better than that?*

"To make things even more exciting," Jasmine continues, "I'd like to introduce our guest judge for today's challenge." She turns to face a nearby door, and a short, redheaded woman steps out. "Please welcome Mallory Kane, the creator of TooDressy.com. For those of you not familiar with the site, it's a rental-clothing business. The winner of this challenge will not only have his or her design added to the site — it will also be showcased as the formal piece of the month."

Daphne and I exchange excited looks. Holy cow! My best friend, Alex, and I are obsessed with that site. They have the most amazing designer pieces at, like, a fraction of the cost. To have my design be one of the choices? That would be unbelievable.

Missy seems to sense our excitement. "There are definitely perks to this challenge, but it won't be easy," she says. "Take your time examining the items in front of you. Think about what you like and what you don't."

The rest of the designers and I immediately make a beeline for the rack of dresses. Some are smooth and velvety while others are made of satin, silk, taffeta, and spandex. I try to take in all the colors — from the obnoxious ones covered in bling to the muted taupes.

At least there's stuff to work with, I think. With a few design tweaks, I could probably transform these into something wearable.

After a few minutes, Hunter calls us back from the racks. "I hope you had some time to think of a vision for your design," he begins, smiling slyly.

Something about his smile tells me my confidence might have been premature.

"Each of these ensembles has the potential to become something beautiful," Hunter continues, "if you go on what you see, that is."

What else would I go on? I think. Ugh. I hate it when the judges are cryptic. I glance at over at Nina, Derek, Shane, and Daphne, but they look confused too.

"For this challenge," Jasmine says, taking the lead on the explanation, "you will have to remake one of the pieces on the rack into something that would be wearable and fashionable by today's standards."

I can see everyone relax. That's exactly what I was thinking. But then Jasmine, Hunter, and Missy walk up to the racks and start turning everything inside out.

What are they doing? I wonder.

"The hard part," says Missy with a grin, "is that you will have to transform the dress or suit as seen from the inside out."

I put my head in my hands. Suddenly an entire day of designing and sewing doesn't seem like enough time at all. What am I going to do with the seams? How will I get the fabric to look how I want? I think, feeling panicky.

It's not just me. Shane looks shell-shocked. Even usually confident and upbeat Derek seems a little thrown by the challenge. Suddenly my dreams of making it to the top three seem farther away than ever.

For the first time, when the judges start the clock, the usual scramble for fabric and materials doesn't happen. No one races to the racks. In fact, no one moves. We all just stare at the clothes in front of us, not sure how to begin.

Does it even matter which dress I pick anymore? I think. The concept is so far beyond the fabric and style.

"Hey," says Liesel, moving to stand at my side. "What are you thinking?"

"That this is impossible," I mutter. I notice a cameraman moving closer and avert my gaze. The last thing I need is for my self-doubt to be broadcast on national television.

Liesel looks at her watch. "I'll give you five minutes of self-defeatist thoughts — then you have to plan. Deal?"

I smile. "Deal." Maybe that's all I need, I think. To flush out the bad thoughts and then get to work.

But somehow knowing I have permission to wallow makes it harder to do so. My mind starts drifting to the dresses and what I can do to transform them into something wearable. Do I want short or long? Crinkly or not? Tight or loose?

Liesel hasn't called time on my wallowing, but I'm over it. I decide to go for an in-between option and create an asymmetrical hemline. I head back to the rack of dresses and settle on a long one with puffy sleeves and a gold sash. It is about three sizes too big, but the bright emerald green color is so striking I can't resist. Plus there are minimal seams to deal with, so I grab my sketchpad and start brainstorming.

Liesel peers over my shoulder at my sketches and nods approvingly. "See, I knew you could do it. That looks great. It's a really modern take on that dress."

Suddenly Hunter appears by my side. And he's not alone — a camera crew is right there with him. "Can you talk us through your vision?" he asks.

"Sure," I say, trying to measure, talk to him, and ignore the cameras at the same time. I make marks by the bust, then put down my fabric pen. Turns out talking and measuring looks a lot easier on television than it is in reality. "My idea is to cut strips from the gold sash and use them to cover the seams." From the corner of my eye, I see Nina stop what she's doing to listen in. "I have some cool ideas for the hem and sleeves, too, but I'd like to keep those a surprise."

Hunter nods. "A little mystery is always good," he agrees. "I look forward to seeing what you come up with."

Nina frowns but puts on a happy face as soon as Hunter and the camera crew move in her direction. I don't bother trying to eavesdrop on what she's saying — I already have my design plan in place. Hearing her plans will just psych me out.

I slip the dress over the top of my dress form and start pinning the waist and bust to take it in. I work along the existing side seams, then measure where the new hem will be. I'll have to take off quite a bit of length to make the dress wearable, but the new hemline will be a modern twist on the dress, and the volume will help balance the tight waistline I'm envisioning.

Once I've cut off the bottom half of the dress, as well as the puffy sleeves, I head over to the sewing machine and get to work taking the dress in. Soon I lose myself in the rhythmic hum of the sewing machine. I take my time, making sure my sewing is clean and precise. I don't

COLOR PALETTE:
EMERALD GREEN
& GOLD

need something like that tripping me up at this stage in the competition.

Once the dress is a more manageable size, I slip it back over my dress form. I still need to add a hidden side zipper, but I'll do that once I've added the fabric strips to define the waist.

Grabbing the gold sash that went with the original dress, I measure out strips of fabric several inches wide, making sure they're long enough to wrap around the natural waist of my dress. When I have the strips ready, I brush hair out of my face and step back to get a better look at what I have so far.

"Nice work," says Liesel. "Want to break for lunch?"

I look at my watch and am surprised to see I've been at it for three hours. I stretch my hands behind my back and shake out my legs, only now noticing how cramped they are from crouching. "In another hour?" I suggest. "I want to get the metallic strips started before I take a break."

Liesel smiles, and I can tell she's proud of me. "You haven't even asked for my help!" she says.

"There's still time," I say. For now, I'm on a roll.

* * *

The rest of the time flies by. I've crisscrossed the gold strips at the natural waist of the dress, and they're the perfect accent. The metallic fabric contrasts with the gorgeous emerald material on the rest of the dress, and I've sewn the strips on the bias to make them more flattering. Now they emphasize the waist perfectly and help disguise the exposed seams.

I've also eliminated the poufy sleeves of the dress and altered the neckline. Nothing too severe — just an elegant boatneck. The higher neckline helps balance out the newly shortened, asymmetrical hem. The overall effect changes the dress from an eighties-themed monstrosity into a sleek, modern gown.

But with only an hour left on the clock, my nerves start to set in. I still need to make some last-minute tweaks, like adding the hidden zipper to the side and fixing the hemline. It looks a little crooked right now, and I know that won't fly with the judges.

"What can I do to help?" Liesel asks.

"Sew for me?" I say hopefully. But I know that's the one thing Liesel can't do. Advise? Yes. Explain? Sure. Do my project for me? A big fat no. "Just kidding," I say. "What do you think it needs?"

"I think you need to take the hem out and redo it over here," Liesel says, voicing exactly what I was thinking.

"The whole thing?" I say. I immediately feel panicky. "How am I going to finish everything if I have to redo the hem?"

"You're not undoing the entire thing," Liesel says. "It'll only require minimal sewing to fix it. Trust me."

I do. It's why she's gotten this far. I reach for the seam ripper that was in my basket, but it's not there. "Where'd my seam ripper go?" I ask. "It was just here."

Liesel rummages through my scraps. "Are you sure?" she asks.

"Yes." I get on my hands and knees but don't see it anywhere.

"Forget it," says Liesel. "Get another one."

"But it was just here," I insist.

Liesel ignores me and grabs another seam ripper. I try to push the missing seam ripper out of my head as I undo the stitching. Lining the hem up carefully to make sure it's even and straight this time, I sew it back into place. "Done!"

Just then, Nina turns toward me, and I notice a second seam ripper in the basket at her feet. "Why do you have two?" I ask.

"Two what?" Nina replies innocently.

"Seam rippers." I look at the handles. Mine definitely had a blue handle, just like the extra one by Nina's feet.

Nina shrugs as the camera crew, sensing some growing tension, surrounds us. "I don't know," she says. "It must have rolled over here."

"Yeah, from my basket!" I can't keep my voice down.

"Don't blame me if you can't keep track of your stuff, Chloe," Nina snaps, turning away.

"Can't keep track of my—" I want to lunge at her.

"Forget it, Chloe," says Liesel, gently tugging on my arm. "You don't have much time left. Focus on your design."

I know Liesel is right, but it's hard to focus when I'm so frustrated. And worst of all, the cameras are right there recording everything. It's going to look like I totally lost my cool — I can only hope they don't edit it to make me look too crazy.

"Santa Cruz friendship torn apart by seam ripper!" I imagine the *Design Diva* commercials saying. Not that there ever was a friendship.

With a final sigh, I turn away from the cameras to put the finishing touches on my dress. I refuse to let Nina's underhanded tactics take this away from me.

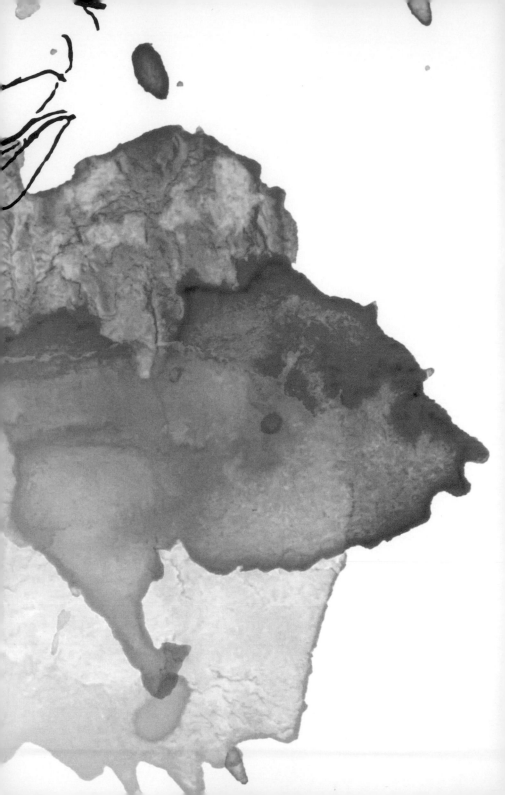

When the judges call time, I'm ready. The other contestants and I take our spots next to our mannequins for the judging process, and I try to focus on how pretty my dress turned out instead of worrying about my earlier freak-out.

Surprisingly, Derek and Shane both opted to create menswear-inspired designs. Menswear isn't exactly my strong suit, but I'm definitely impressed. It's a totally different take on the challenge. I almost wish one of their designs could be chosen in addition to one of the dresses Nina, Daphne, and I created.

The judges begin their short walk around our creations. For a several minutes, no one says anything. Then Mallory Kane suddenly claps her hands. "Bravo!" she shouts. "I have to confess something. When I agreed to be a part of this show, I was pretty nervous about what that would mean. I've seen *Design Diva*, and some of the visions are . . . well, let's just say different from mine. I was a little worried about what I would do if I had to choose from a group of out-there designs."

Well, this is a great pep talk, I think. *Is she going to tell us how terrible she finds all our designs?*

Then Mallory smiles. "But you've all surprised me. There's not just one design I'd be happy to display on my site — I'd love to see all of your work displayed." She frowns. "That's what makes judging so difficult."

Mallory walks around each design for the second time. When she's done pacing, she claps her hands again. "That's it!" she yells. "I've got the solution!"

Jasmine, Missy, and Hunter look alarmed. Whatever is coming was clearly not scripted. "Maybe we should talk about—" Hunter starts to say.

But Mallory doesn't let him finish. "My site, my rules," she interrupts. "I've decided that instead of just one contestant's design being showcased, I want to display two. One menswear-inspired item and one dress."

The judges quickly glance at the cameras, and their plastic smiles immediately return. "What a lovely idea!" Missy says.

"What a treat for everyone!" Jasmine agrees through clenched teeth.

Derek and Shane grin at each other. I can understand their excitement. Mallory's decision to change the rules must mean she likes at least one of their designs enough to keep it in the running.

"Let's start by discussing what we like about each design," Hunter says, sounding rushed.

He probably wants to get started before Mallory tries to change anything else, I think.

"Great idea," Missy says. "Nina, let's start with you. I like how you utilized satin to create a mermaid-style dress. The flared lower half really shows your command of sewing skills."

My body tenses. Nina used satin? That has to give her points since it's pretty challenging to work with.

"Thank you," Nina says. Her smile looks a little smug to me, and I have to resist the urge to roll my eyes. "I was really inspired by old Hollywood glamour."

"I like the mermaid style, too," says Jasmine. "And using satin is a bold choice." She pauses to examine the stitching of the satin and nods. "However, I can see you had some trouble with it here, here, and here."

Nina's face reddens with embarrassment, and she doesn't say anything.

"Overall, though, fine work," Hunter says. "You can barely tell this dress has been turned inside out."

"Thanks," Nina mumbles. She looks over at her mentor and then looks away again. Tanya looks irritated, but it's impossible to tell if her frustration is directed at the judges or at Nina.

Daphne is up next. "I chose a white dress," she explains, "and dyed it to create an ombré effect. I also altered the back of the dress. It was a scoop neck before, so I made it just a little bit deeper and more dramatic."

"I love this color!" Mallory gushes. "You've done such a fantastic job with the dyeing."

"I agree," says Hunter. "The color is spot on. And I love the fabric, but it seems like that's really all you did. I'd have liked to see more complexity in the design itself. It's a bit too basic for my tastes. There's no real risk."

Daphne's face falls as the judges move on to the boys. Shane chose to go with a less-traditional suit style with pants that fall just below the knees. Derek's suit pants fall past the ankles. He also made a vest from the excess fabric, adding gold buttons to the front and creating a vertical striped design with gold thread.

"The tailoring on both of these suits is very impressive," Mallory says. "I wish we could use all of these." She swipes at her eyes.

OTHER CONTESTANTS' *Designs*

SHANE'S SUIT
CROPPED PANTS WITH JACKET

DEREK'S SUIT
MENSWEAR INSPIRED

"I agree with you on the tailoring," Jasmine interrupts, "but, Shane, these cropped pants are just oddly proportioned. The length of the pants isn't flattering with the blazer, and they don't really work with the overall suit design."

Shane frowns but doesn't say anything as the judges move in my direction.

"My favorite aspect of this dress," says Mallory, jumping right into her critique, "is the asymmetrical hem. It adds just the right amount of interest to the dress."

I hardly have time to enjoy the compliment before Jasmine jumps in. "My concern is whether or not this style will withstand the test of time," she says. "It's stylish now, but the mark of a lasting design is something that can be worn for more than a month. This is awfully trendy."

I notice Nina winking at Tanya, and I clench my fists.

"Still," says Missy, "I love the bold color. It's just stunning. And the bands of contrasting fabric around the middle are beautiful. The fabric strips are very slimming, and I adore the metallic accents. You can't tell this dress was inside out."

Jasmine glares at Missy. *What's the problem?* I wonder. Maybe it makes for bad television if the judges leave us

feeling confident about our design. Have to keep the audience — and us — guessing, I suppose.

"As Mallory said, everyone's designs today were impressive. It's clear you've all come a long way since this competition started," Hunter says. "And even though we'd like to keep you all, two designers will be going home today. When we come back, we'll reveal who will be advancing to the top three."

With that, the judges disappear. Everyone seems nervous. Daphne is looking at the ground, and I see Nina biting her fingernails. Even if she did steal my seam ripper, there's something about her hunched posture and nervous biting that make me feel sorry for her. Shane looks to the judging room, then back to his design. Even though I like his suit, he hasn't seemed the same since his brother was sent home.

I don't see Derek, but suddenly I feel a tap on my shoulder, and he's standing right behind me. "I really liked your dress," he says.

"Thanks," I say, feeling flattered. "I've liked all your designs from the start. The stuff you came up with for the rodeo challenge back in Salinas was awesome!"

Derek blushes. Sensing a moment he might need to capture, one of the cameramen gets closer. Derek rolls his eyes. "That's right, folks," he says to the cameras.

"We're forming an alliance. Or are we?" He wiggles his eyebrows, and I laugh. The cameraman moves on to Shane.

"I guess we don't provide enough drama," I say.

Derek rolls his eyes again. "Fine by me," he says. "I've been trying to lie low and avoid that."

Before I can reply, the judges reappear. That didn't take long.

"We've come to our decision," Jasmine announces. "While we agree each of the designs is special, we can only choose three to move on to the final round of the competition."

"I want to emphasize, however," Missy jumps in, as Jasmine rolls her eyes, "that we are all so impressed with how far you've come. Don't let tonight's elimination detract from everything you've accomplished."

"While all five of you did great work, two of your designs really stood out," Mallory says. "They are not only stylish, but I can see them being popular for years to come."

My heart sinks. Jasmine made it *more* than clear that she didn't think my dress would stand the test of time. Mallory's statement seems like foreshadowing — even if I make it to the top three, my dress won't be featured on her site.

"Derek," Mallory says, "your command of fabric, stitching, and color makes your feminine suit a welcome addition to any wardrobe."

Derek takes a deep breath. There always seems to be a but following the judges' compliments — but not this time.

"Congratulations!" Mallory exclaims. "Your suit is the top menswear-inspired pick for my site!"

"Daphne, Shane, Nina, and Chloe," Hunter says, taking over, "only two of you will continue on in the competition after today. Nina, your mermaid dress was an interesting silhouette, and we were impressed by your choice of fabrics. You're safe."

I see Nina let out a huge sigh of relief. From the sidelines, Tanya gives her a proud smile and a big thumbs-up.

"We have one spot left in our final three," Jasmine says. "Chloe, I had questioned whether your dress would still be something teens would want to wear in the future."

Instinctively, I glance over at the camera. "Yes," I say. "I remember." The knot in my stomach gets tighter.

"I agree with Mallory that the design will appeal for many seasons," says Jasmine. "Sorry to keep you hanging like that."

It takes me a minute to make sense of what Jasmine said. "You mean I'm safe?" I ask. I can hardly believe it. I made it to the final three!

"You're more than safe," Mallory says. "You're also our other winner. Your dress will be featured on my website. Congratulations!"

I gasp. This is too good to be true. "Thank you," I manage to say.

"Unfortunately, Daphne and Shane, that means you'll both be leaving us today," Jasmine says. "We've enjoyed your designs throughout the competition, but this round they weren't where they needed to be to move on. We wish you both the best."

Shane and Daphne take the elimination better than expected, hugging everyone goodbye before leaving the room. Then there are three — Nina, Derek, and me.

Derek hugs me, but Nina hangs back until Tanya whispers something in her ear. Then, she gingerly puts her arms around me and offers a forced smile for the cameras. I close my eyes, and this time the dresses of my nightmare are gone. All I see now is row after row of my emerald dress.

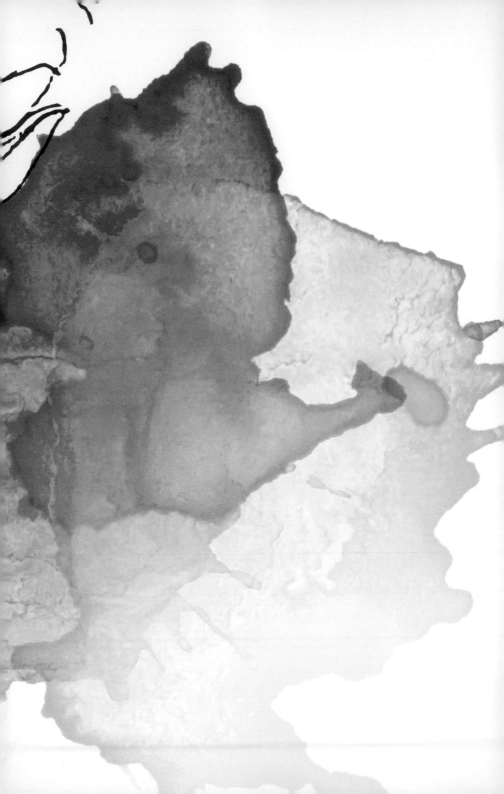

The night before the final challenge, I try to focus on relaxing. The internship is almost in my hands, and I don't want to psych myself out. I sprawl on the hotel bed and flip through the channels until I come across the most recent episode of *Teen Design Diva*. It's the dress challenge. They're breaking it up into two parts, with the results show airing at the end of the week.

I watch as the commercials tease what will happen in tonight's episode. They show me on my hands and knees looking for the seam ripper. Then they show me yelling at Nina and the screen freezes on my angry face. Just as the voiceover says, "Has the pressure finally gotten to be too much for one of the designers?" my phone rings.

"What the heck?" Alex says before I even manage to say hello.

"It wasn't my fault," I tell her. "You'll see."

"Duh," Alex says. "I'm your best friend. I know that. What did Nina do?"

"I don't know for sure if she did anything," I say. "I just have my suspicions. Let's just watch. You'll find out when I do."

The show does a montage of all the contestants before launching into the instructions for the challenge. There's my relieved face when we're told about the extra time and help from our mentors. The camera stays on me as we're told about the inside-out twist, and I frown with worry. My nervous face is the last thing viewers see before the commercial break.

"I think they're trying to show your descent into madness," Alex says with a laugh.

"Drama," I say, groaning.

When the show returns, they've switched gears. The cameras zoom in on Shane and Daphne, both hard at work. Hunter says something to Shane that we can't hear, and Shane nods. Then the show cuts to a confessional of Shane.

"I'm kind of done," Shane admits to the camera. "Without Sam here . . . I don't know. That really got to me. I'm doing my best, but honestly I'll be fine if I go home tonight."

"No!" Alex shouts in my ear. "Tell me he doesn't get eliminated."

"You know I can't tell you that," I say. "You have to watch to find out."

Alex grumbles, and the cameras move over to Nina, who is deep in discussion with her mentor. "I'm doing the best I can!" Nina snaps at Tanya over the top of her sewing machine.

I have to admit, Nina does seem to be working hard. Her fingers are moving quickly, and unlike mine, her basket and scraps are well organized. Hunter walks over to her to discuss the design she's working on, but before he can say anything Nina shakes her head. "I'm sorry. I'm just too swamped to talk."

I can practically hear Alex rolling her eyes through the phone. "I can't believe her nerve. All hail, Queen Nina," she mutters.

The camera pans back to me. My back is to my basket as I sew the fabric strips around the waist of my dress. That's when I see it. Nina stealthily walks over to my basket and takes the seam ripper.

"Oh, no she didn't!" Alex exclaims. "Why is she taking your stuff?"

I'm too busy watching to answer her. I suspected this, and seeing it actually take place makes me angry all over again. The camera pans back to Tanya, who gives Nina a quick high-five. It stays on the pair, and I turn up the volume.

"That's how to do it," Tanya says under her breath. "If you really want to win, you have to prove it. You have to be willing to do anything."

Nina is back at her machine and grinning. "I do want it," she says. "I gave her this hideous necklace while we were back home, too, and told her that's what the judges are looking for."

"Nice," Tanya says with a smirk "Maybe she'll use it in the finale."

"What a jerk!" shouts Alex. "If you're in the finale, you should use that necklace. You can make anything look amazing."

I stare at the screen, not saying anything. Even though I suspected Nina wasn't playing fair, seeing proof of it stinks. Her elbowing me in the side early on in the competition clearly wasn't an accident. Neither was my seam ripper going missing. And now the necklace.

I don't want to watch the rest of the show. I already know I freaked out on her. I don't need to watch the replay on national television.

"I'll talk to you tomorrow, Alex," I say. "Keep watching. It gets good."

I hang up, suddenly exhausted. I know Nina wants to win, but so do I. It's like elementary school all over again. The only difference is me. When I was a kid, I would've cowered and let her win.

Not this time, I think determinedly. *I'll do exactly what Alex said. Not only will I find a way to use that ugly necklace, I'll win with it.*

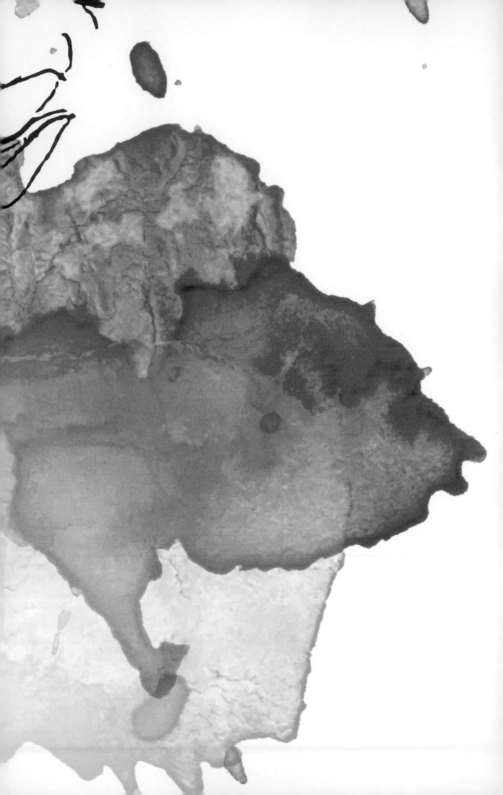

44

The final challenge is being held in a huge conference room in the hotel. Today, it's relatively empty — just us, the judges, the producers, and the camera crew. On Monday, it will be packed for the live finale.

"Designers," Missy says, "welcome to the final challenge! As we mentioned earlier on in the competition, for this challenge, you'll each be allowed to use one item from home. Do you all have yours?"

I pat my pocket with the necklace Nina gave me back in California. That feels so long ago at this point.

Missy continues. "It's been a long road, and for one of you, the journey will continue. As you know, the prize for winning this challenge, and the show, is an amazing fashion internship."

My heart is beating fast, and I feel my blood pumping. The internship is almost within reach. I can't believe how far I've come since the first challenge. But I still have one final challenge to go. And Derek is a great designer. So is Nina — as much it pains me to admit it.

"For your final task," Jasmine says, "you will have to create an outfit that can do double duty. It must be something that could be worn in the office, as well as for any evening events."

"You will have until five p.m. Friday night to complete this challenge," says Missy. "That's almost two and a half days, so we expect to see your best. Your time starts now!"

I take a deep breath and focus on the challenge at hand. With so many hours to complete a task, I know I'll need a design that's extra special. I think of office wear that's inspired me in the past, and the perfect idea forms in my mind — a sheath dress with a slim pencil skirt. It'll be perfect for the workplace during the day, especially if I add a removable collar. To transform it into something I could wear to an event, I'll add a peplum ruffle at the waist that can be zipped on or off. With the peplum on and the collar off, it'll be a chic party dress. I'll use a rayon-nylon-spandex blend for the dress and silk-cotton shirting for the collar and peplum.

Versatile:
Work to Gala

REMOVABLE
DESIGN IDEAS:
• ZIPPER ATTACHMENTS
• PEPLUM RUFFLE

INTERNSHIP
DEVELOPMENT
Sketches

TOOLS OF THE TRADE

• Thread
• Fabric
• Accents
• Snaps
• Zipper

It'll be a lot of work, but I need something big. At this point in the competition, it's go big or go home. And going home was never part of my plan.

* * *

"Talk us through your design so far," Hunter says later that afternoon. He motions for the camera crew to move closer.

I sigh. I may have gotten used to having the cameras around, but it doesn't mean I like them. "I'm creating a sheath dress with a natural waist for the office," I explain. "The definition at the waist and fitted skirt will make it office appropriate, and I have some removable accents to help transform the dress depending on where it'll be worn." I attempt to sew while talking but give up.

"Sounds like you have a lot of work ahead of you," Hunter says.

I smile. "Yep, so if you don't mind . . ." I trail off.

Hunter laughs and motions for the cameras to follow him to Nina. "I can take a hint. Best of luck, Chloe."

Once he leaves, I finish marking the pattern on my fabric. I've opted for basic black for my sheath dress. Some people might think it's too boring, but to me, it screams simple and chic. The black-and-white combo will look elegant and modern, like a feminine tuxedo. Best of all, I'm staying true to my style aesthetic. I might get brave and branch out with color on occasion, but for a big challenge like this, I'm sticking with what I know.

Once I have my pattern set, I grab my fabric and head over to my sewing machine to start sewing.

"Use this," says Derek, suddenly beside me, tissue paper in hand. "If you put it under the fabric, it will keep it in place while you sew."

I have to admit, I'm surprised by the gesture. "Helping the competition?" I say with a laugh. "Viewers will love that."

Derek shakes his head. "I don't care about that. If I beat you, I want it to be the best you. Otherwise, how will I know where I stand?"

Even when he's not sewing, Derek impresses me. I don't see myself doing the same for Nina. "Thanks," I say gratefully. Out of the corner of my eye, I see Nina's shocked face. Clearly, she wouldn't do the same for me either.

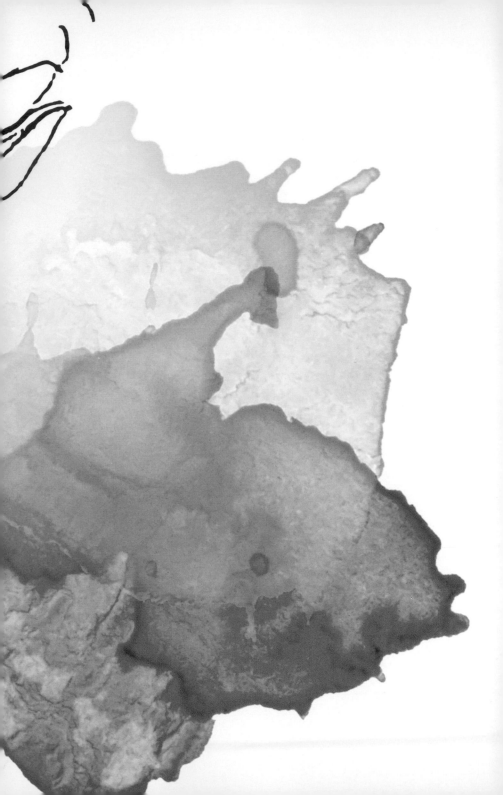

45

As the day continues, I only take a few small breaks. Some water here, a sandwich there, and it's back to the machine. I don't have any time to waste if I want to finish my dress in time.

It's past nine when Jasmine walks over to my station. "Interesting choice of material," she says. From her tone of voice it's impossible to tell if she means interesting in a good way or a bad way. But at this point, I don't have time to redo it either way.

Jasmine keeps inspecting my work so far, focusing on the seams, while I watch nervously. I've tapered the waist and added darts to my dress to make it more slimming. "It looks like you've made some major improvements from the shift dress we saw from you back in the first round of auditions," she finally says.

"Derek gave me a few tips," I say.

Jasmine raises her eyebrows. "It's a welcome change to see camaraderie in this competition." Did she just give Nina a pointed look?

Jasmine moves on to Derek, and I can hear her fawning over his design. It's clear from the tone of her voice that she's impressed. As usual, his construction is spot on. I don't want to wish bad luck on anyone, but would it be too much to ask for him to flub his stitching just once?

I keep working. I can't let myself get rattled by the competition. At this point, it's anyone's game, so I need to be at my best. Only a few more stitches before I call it a night. Tomorrow, I need to work on tailoring the dress and creating the removable collar and peplum piece. I still need to figure out how to incorporate the clunky chain Nina gave me, too. I'm determined to use it somehow.

I sew my last stitch and see Derek and Nina packing it up for the night too. From what I can see of their designs so far, they're determined to bring their "A" game to the final challenge as well. For the first time today, I notice the ache in my fingers and shoulders. The pain is a comforting reminder of all the hard work I put in.

* * *

The next morning we're back in the workroom bright and early. The camera lights seem brighter today, and my fingers feel less able. I knew yesterday's Zen feeling was too good to be true. Last night, it seemed like I had all the time in the world to finish my design. But today has been full of nothing but stitching mishaps — or at least that's how it feels. My thread keeps breaking, and my rushed fingers mess up even zigzag stitches. Oversleeping this morning didn't help either. Now, it's after eight at night, and I'm still trying to put the finishing touches on my dress.

Just ignore the cameras, I tell myself. I take a deep breath and slip the lining inside my dress, like I'm placing one tube inside another. I sew around the top edge of the neckline, then carry my dress over to the sewing machine to hem it. Once it's done, I slip it back on my dress form to keep the fabric from getting wrinkled. I still need to attach Nina's chain necklace, which I've decided to use as a belt, but I don't want to do it while she's around, so I decide to focus on my removable pieces instead.

As the clock strikes ten, I grab the silk-cotton shirting I'll be using to create my peplum ruffle. Sleep

363

beckons, but I push the thought away. Why save anything for tomorrow? A cameraman yawns silently and trails after me.

"Calling it a night soon?" Missy asks. She looks as tired as I feel.

"Almost," I say.

"Good luck," Missy says. "And remember that no matter what happens, we're all proud of you."

I sit at my machine and think about what she just said. No matter what happens? What does that mean? Is she trying to let me down easy already? Does she think those words lessen the blow of losing? Let's face it, at this point in the competition, no one is going to be happy to come in second.

Trying to put Missy's words out of my mind, I get to work on the peplum, measuring the waist of my dress form and calculating how large of an opening I'll need to cut in the fabric to make it fit. I fold the fabric in half twice, creating four layers, then cut the correct amount out of one corner to create an even loop of fabric.

I hold the fabric up against my dress to figure out how I want it to look. Then I cut out another long strip of white material. Laying it out, I pin it and use a fabric marker to trace along the edge of where I want it placed. Then I unpin it and cut the material out. I add a few small stitches down along the two ruffled areas on the front of the peplum to reinforce them, then place the long strip around the peplum, pin it, and sew it in place.

I hand sew a couple of hook-and-eye closures to the dress and peplum piece so it can be easily removed, then stand back to admire my work. It's one of my best designs yet — I just hope it's enough. I can already imagine myself walking the streets of New York in it, sitting in meetings with fashion executives, and discussing the latest designs.

I place the dress in a garment bag and hang it beside Nina's and Derek's bags. I know their designs are probably their best work too. Thinking back on all the different challenges, it's almost impossible to tell who will win tomorrow. Nina and I have been pretty closely matched throughout the competition, while Derek has been at the front of the pack since week one. I can only hope the judges will see how much I've improved and how much effort I put into my dress. With the internship so close, there's no room for mistakes.

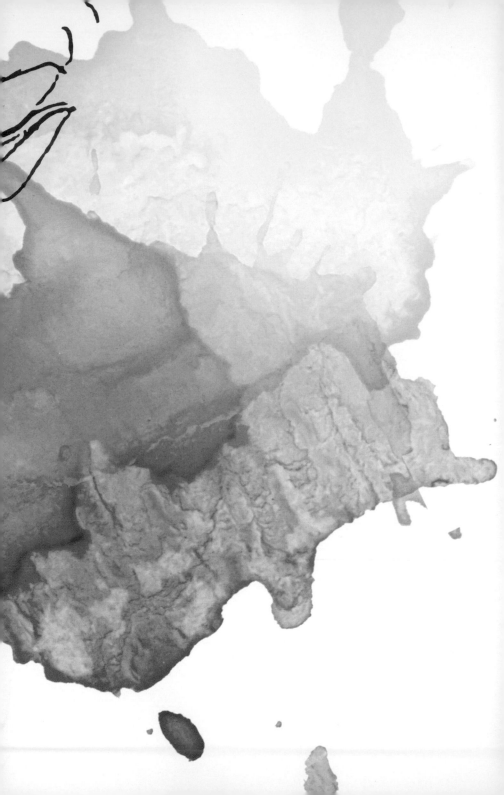

Monday is chaos as our family members are flown in from around the country and the stage is set up for the big finale. Unlike earlier in the week, every seat in the room is filled with family members, friends, past contestants, and other viewers. Liesel is there — and so is Jake. I haven't seen him since I visited Liesel's store for inspiration, but he's as cute as I remember.

"Break a needle," my dad tells me before he goes to find a seat in the audience beside my mom. I've missed him so much these past few weeks — even his corny jokes.

I laugh. "That's not even a saying! But thanks."

Liesel and Jake walk up to the stage, and Liesel gives me a hug. "I'm so proud to have been your mentor, Chloe," she says. "Knock them dead."

Jake gives me a hug too, and I blush. "You're going to kill it out there," he says.

Just then, a producer comes over and ushers me to the stage so we can get started. Nina and Derek are already there, standing beside their dress forms. The lights dim, and Hunter takes the stage. "Welcome, everyone, to the finale of *Teen Design Diva!*" he says, and the audience cheers. "All the contestants have come so far. Let's watch their journeys."

A video montage starts up, chronicling clips of us throughout the series. The clips from the show are interwoven with interviews with our family, friends, and other people from back home. I shoot a surprised look at the audience. I didn't know they interviewed our family and friends.

I get to see Derek's house. His mom shows off his room, which is lined wall-to-wall with his designs. Apparently, he's one of six kids and captain of his school's swim and baseball teams. The producers interview his teammates about what a team player he is before moving on to a montage of his wins throughout the show.

Nina's video shows her gaggle of followers back in Santa Cruz. They're all giggling as they fawn over how wonderful Nina is. Then the video shows her house, where her mom talks about how helpful Nina is, finding time to help around the house when she's not busy designing.

Huh. I never pegged her as the helpful type, I think. The video zooms through the challenges. First, Nina's rodeo-inspired design, then the zoo competition, and finally the team challenge.

Then it's my turn. My video shows my parents and Alex talking about how much I love designing and how long I've been doing it. The producers show the outside of Mimi's Thrifty Threads and interview Mimi, who calls me talented and creative. There's a clip of me talking about my gramps during the audition process. Watching myself choke up on screen makes my cheeks flush, but I watch proudly. My grandpa's inspiration helped put me on this show. There are clips of me being named to the top fifteen, my toy store challenge win, and the Sony Wonder Lab.

When the video ends, Missy steps forward. "There's no doubt you'll be seeing all three of these talented designers for years to come," she says. "Remember, you saw them here first!"

The crowd cheers, and Jasmine raises her hands in the air for silence. "Tonight, however, is about choosing one winner. One of these designers will win the opportunity of a lifetime — an internship with a top designer here in

New York and the chance to take the fashion world by storm. Let's get started."

The judges make their way to where Derek is standing. "Can you talk us through your design?" Jasmine asks.

"I'd love to," Derek says with a charming smile. "I wanted something easy and effortless; I think everyone wants to look good at work without having to put too much thought into it. So I chose to create a shirtdress with a cropped blazer. Both pieces work individually or as a complete outfit."

The judges examine Derek's shirtdress by itself for a moment, and then Derek adds the black blazer to the ensemble, transforming it into eveningwear. Like with all of Derek's designs, the blazer has minute, intricate additions like embroidery on the lapels.

Hunter nods. "I love the gold accents on both pieces. The gold buttons on the shirtdress coordinate nicely with the embroidery on the blazer's lapel. I might be calling you for ideas sometime."

"Anytime," Derek says with a wink at the audience. "I'm happy to share."

"Fantastic," says Missy before moving over to Nina.

Even though I can't stand her at the moment, I have to admit Nina's design is stunning. She went for a vintage

OTHER CONTESTANTS' *Designs*

DEREK'S INTERN LOOK
SHIRTDRESS WITH CROPPED BLAZER

NINA'S INTERN LOOK
1950S-INSPIRED DRESS
WITH BLAZER FOR DAY

1950s feel with a strapless, cinched-waist dress. Pink lace covers the fitted bust and a darker satin belt connects it to the flared-out black satin skirt.

"The dress is adorable!" Missy exclaims, echoing my thoughts. "But how would you make it appropriate for the office?"

Nina adds an open-front black blazer she's holding on her arm. "Adding a tailored jacket takes the dress from event-worthy to something that would fit in at any fashion internship," she says with a smile.

"Just lovely," says Missy. "Thank you."

I take a deep breath as the judges make their way toward me. "Last, but not least," Hunter says with a smile. "Chloe, tell us about your dress, please."

"I really wanted to stick with my simple-chic style aesthetic," I say. "After all, that's what got me this far. So I decided to create a tailored shift dress in a monochromatic color palette. I used black rayon for the majority of the dress and a silk-cotton shirting for the collar. Metallic accents help add some shine and a throwback to some of my earlier designs."

Missy comes closer and examines the chunky belt circling the natural waist of the dress — Nina's necklace. I waited until just before the live show to add it to my outfit. "This belt is really interesting," she says. "I love the contrast between the chunky chain and simple lines of the dress."

"That used to be a necklace," I tell her. "Nina kindly bought it for me."

Nina gasps.

"Very chic," says Jasmine. "But as elegant and well-tailored as this dress is, I'm not sure I see it being appropriate for an evening party."

"I'm glad you brought that up," I say, pulling out the peplum piece I created. I take the collar off the dress and slide the peplum around the waist. "These removable pieces make it easy to take the dress from day to night. With some metallic heels and cool jewelry, it will fit in at any event."

"Very impressive, Chloe," Jasmine says. "I love the modern addition of the peplum and that you stayed true to your personal style. You've really created a cohesive collection throughout this competition."

"Ladies and gentlemen," says Hunter, "I'm sure you're as blown away with these final designs as we are. But you'll have to wait until after the commercial break to find out which designer takes it all."

"And five, four, three, two, one!" the producer counts down.

Jasmine steps up to the mic as soon as the commercial segment ends. "It's been a long road," she says. "And all three of our designers have grown tremendously throughout this competition. Let's give them one final round of applause."

The crowd claps and whistles. When they settle down, Jasmine continues. "We won't be criticizing anyone's design today because they are all fantastic. What it came down to for us was who took that extra step."

That could mean anything. Derek's shirtdress and jacket were high quality and well made. As much as I hate to admit it, Nina's dress was adorable. I still like my dress the best, but that doesn't mean the judges did. It's anyone's game.

"Who has consistently improved throughout the competition and grown as a designer," adds Hunter.

"The winner of the first season of *Teen Design Diva* and recipient of the fashion internship in New York City is . . ." Missy pauses. "Chloe Montgomery!"

Balloons fall from the ceiling and confetti rains down around me. I feel like I'm in a fog.

It's me, right?

They said my name?

My family, Jake, and Liesel rush to the stage. My mom and dad hug and swing me around.

"I knew you could do it, Chloe," my dad whispers in my ear.

"We're so proud of you, honey!" my mom exclaims, grinning at me.

Someone taps me on the shoulder, and I turn to see Derek standing there. "I'm rethinking helping you now," he says with a grin. "Kidding. You deserve it. Your design really was the best one."

"Thanks," I say, still shocked. "Your stuff has always been amazing."

"Thanks," Derek says. "Congrats again. I'll see you around."

Derek heads offstage, and I catch Nina's eye. "Good work," she mutters grudgingly before rushing off the stage too.

The judges hug me. "You've come so far, girl," says Jasmine. "I can't wait to see what's next for you."

That's a real compliment coming from Jasmine. She must believe in tough love.

The world is spinning. A cameraman shoves through the crowd as Hunter hands me a mic. "What are you feeling, Chloe? Did you have any idea you'd make it this far?"

"I'm feeling awed," I say. "Shocked. This is unbelievable. Who wouldn't be thrilled to have this opportunity? To answer your second question, it took me a while to believe in myself, but I'm very lucky to have supportive friends and family."

I think of Mimi back home. Without her, there's a good chance I'd still be sitting in my room wondering if I should have entered the competition. I remember my promise to mention her store if I won. "One woman in my town owns a store called Mimi's Thrifty Threads. She has been an amazing inspiration. Look her up!"

Suddenly arms surround me from behind and I'm being picked up and swung through the air. When I'm back on solid ground, I turn around to see Jake standing there. "Congratulations!" he says. He leans in and gives me a kiss on the cheek. "Now that you'll be in New York, I'll get to see even more of you."

The balloons and confetti have stopped falling, but I still feel weightless. Through the window of the room, I see the bright lights of the city and the top of the Empire State Building.

"Chloe," Missy says, appearing at my elbow, "we need you to sign paperwork and meet your internship bosses. There will be a blog, Fashion Week prep, you name it. There's so much to do!"

Missy keeps chattering, and I try to take it all in. I think about all the different versions of who I've been along the way — Confident Chloe, Cowardly Chloe, Charismatic Chloe, Clumsy Chloe. I think of how far I've come.

Cameras flash in my face, but this time, I don't want to run away. I belong here. And I'll tackle everything that lies ahead on my own terms, as myself.

Just Chloe.

That's who I am, and it's enough.

The Author

Margaret Gurevich has wanted to be a writer since second grade. She has written for many magazines and currently writes young-adult and middle-grade books. She loves hiking, cooking, reading, watching too much television, and spending time with her husband and son.

The Illustrator

Brooke Hagel is a fashion illustrator based in New York City. While studying fashion design at the Fashion Institute of Technology, she began her career as an intern, working in the wardrobe department of *Sex and the City*, the design studios of Cynthia Rowley, and the production offices of *Saturday Night Live*. After graduating, Brooke began designing and styling for Hearst Magazines, contributing to *Harper's Bazaar*, *House Beautiful*, *Seventeen*, and *Esquire*. Brooke is now a successful illustrator with clients including *Vogue*, *Teen Vogue*, *InStyle*, Dior, Brian Atwood, Hugo Boss, Barbie, Gap, and Neutrogena.

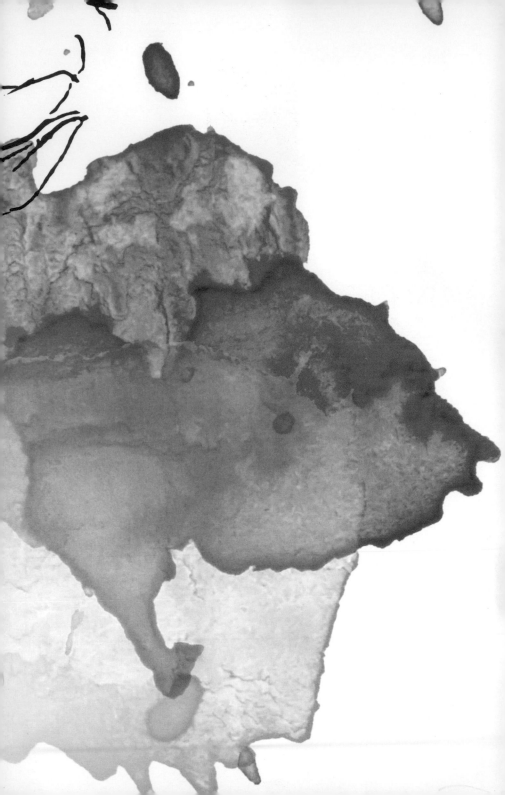